Song of Sula

Lavinia Derwent

Song of Sula

text and cover illustrations by
Prudence Seward

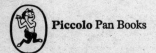
Piccolo Pan Books

First published in Great Britain 1976 by
Victor Gollancz Ltd
This edition published 1977 by Pan Books Ltd,
Cavaye Place, London SW10 9PG
© Lavinia Derwent 1976
© Illustrations Prudence Seward 1976
ISBN 0 330 25203 8
Printed and bound in Great Britain by
Richard Clay (The Chaucer Press) Ltd, Bungay, Suffolk

Contents

1 A Stranger in Sula

Everything was as still as a stone in Sula, as if the little island was asleep. Or waiting for something to happen. True, strange events were about to take place, but who could foresee the future? Not the gulls or guillemots clustering together on the rocks, nor Gran going quietly about her daily tasks. Not even Mr Skinnymalink, the Hermit, who was said to have the seeing eye. What could happen to disturb such a peaceful scene? Sula was the same yesterday, today, and for ever.

Now and then a sheep bleated or a seabird gave a plaintive cry. The seals were sporting themselves in the icy-cold water near the seashore. Now and then another head popped up and a sleek body could be seen turning a somersault. A pale wintry sun lit up the sky but there was little warmth in it. Old Whiskers knew it was no use heaving himself out on to his favourite rock. It would be too cold to lie there. Besides, the boy was away.

The old seal had listened in vain for the familiar strains of the reed-pipe and for Magnus's voice calling, 'Whiskers! Old Whiskers! Come on out. I'm home!'

The seal snuffled with self-pity. Then he gave a grunt as if to assure himself that the boy would come back. Magnus would always return to Sula; so would the sunny days of summer.

The sunny days were a long way off but the boy was coming nearer, returning from his first visit to London. Wonderful though the great city was, it was nothing compared to Sula. London was only a big town. Sula was home, where Gran lived and where Magnus was free to scramble across the rocks, swim with the seals, and draw pictures of puffins in his school jotter.

Sula had always been there in his mind's eye, even when he was in the thick of the London traffic. Soon he would step ashore and see it all in reality. It was like a magnet pulling him back. Already the flag was flying from the turret of Cronan Castle to welcome him and the Duke home.

The proud peacocks were strutting on the overgrown lawn, displaying their tail-feathers. The deer were sprucing up their antlers by rubbing them against the trees; and the old gardener was busy sweeping the last of the leaves from the rutted driveway.

Old Bella, wearing a clean apron, was hovering at the front door, where the Duke's dogs sprawled on the steps. There was a look of dismay on her face as she gazed down the driveway and saw the crowd gathered outside the great gates. Reporters, not only from the *Cronan Chronicle*, but from the big newspapers in Glasgow, Edinburgh, and even some from London, as well as men with microphones and television cameras. A straggle of onlookers had gathered, too, peering through the spars like monkeys in a cage.

'It would be terrible if they got in,' said the old woman anxiously. 'Are you sure the gates are locked?'

The gardener nodded, leaning on his broom. 'I have the key in my pocket.'

Bella's brow was still wrinkled with worry. 'His Grace'll be furious. Can you not send them away?'

'I've tried. They won't go.' Old Dan swept the leaves into a heap and straightened his back. 'It's the Duke's own fault,' he grumbled. 'He should have stayed at home. See what has happened. He's gone to London and made himself famous.'

It was the little Duke's music that had made him famous. His *Sula Symphony* had taken London by storm, winning such praise from the critics that everyone was anxious to interview the composer. Especially now. A blue-blooded Duke returning home in triumph to his crumbling castle.

'Him and his music!' said Bella crossly. 'He should have kept it in the Tower room as he always did. It was that laddie from Sula who egged him on.' Suddenly her voice softened. 'All the same, it'll be nice to see Magnus again.'

Magnus Macduff was sitting beside the Duke in McTear's taxi. It was known locally in Cronan as the rattletrap, though it made less din than His Grace's own motor. Even now, sitting in the back, the Duke was still doing the driving. He shoogled backwards and forwards to help the taxi up a steep incline, he banged on the brakes when they came to a crossing, and toot-tooted at a pedestrian who strayed across their path.

He grinned at Magnus. 'We'll soon be in sight of the castle. Isn't it good to be home, boy?'

'Uh-huh!' said Magnus fervently; but it would be even better when he came in sight of Sula. He gazed ahead and cried, 'The flag's flying!'

'So it is!' The Duke bobbed up and down in his seat like a bouncing ball. Then a look of horror came over his face when he caught sight of the crowd congregated at the gates. 'Who are all these people?' he cried out. 'What are they doing here?'

McTear turned round and told him. 'They'll likely have come to interview you, Your Grace. They'll be wanting to take your photo.'

'What?' shrieked the Duke, slumping down so that he could not be seen. 'Don't let them come near me. Send them away!'

Unlike the Duke, McTear was willing enough to be seen. He straightened his cap, leant out of the taxi and beamed at the cameras. This would be the making of him! He and his taxi would be in all the papers, not to mention on the television screens.

'Keep them away!' screamed the Duke, hiding his head in his arms as if a swarm of stinging bees was after his blood.

'It's okay, Duke,' said Magnus soothingly. He had no wish to face the crowd himself, but he braced himself to lean out of the window and call, 'Go away! The Duke's not speaking!'

The pressmen clustered closer to the taxi and a babble of voices began to ask eager questions.

'Look this way, please.' 'What's your name?' 'Were you in London with the Duke?' 'Smile!' 'Are you the boy from Sula?' 'Tell us about the Duke and his Symphony.' 'Can we get a photograph of him?' 'Come on; give us a break. Ask him to say something.'

'He's not speaking!' said Magnus firmly. Out of the corner of his eye he could see the old gardener making his way down the drive. 'Hurry up, Dan!' he called out. 'Open the gates.'

The rusty gates creaked open and McTear's taxi shot through, leaving the disappointed pressmen clicking their cameras at its back-axle as it went rattling up the bumpy driveway.

'Whewh!' cried the little Duke, surfacing from the floor and mopping his brow with an old silk handkerchief with the Cronan crest in the corner. 'Never again!'

The taxi had scarcely stopped before he dived out and bounded in through the castle door. After a hasty greeting to Bella he hurried up the great stairway, making straight for the sanctuary of the Tower room with the dogs scuttling at his heels.

'Never again!' he repeated, perching like a gnome on his favourite stool. He beamed with delight as he looked around him at all the familiar clutter of schoolboy treasures. Cricket bats, stamp collections, model engines, fiddles, music, old newspapers and butterfly nets. 'Aren't you pleased to be back, Magnus?'

'Ay, I am.'

Magnus took a quick look towards his own tidier room where he did his painting and where he could gaze across the water to Sula, his real home. Tomorrow he would be there.

The telephone kept ringing insistently. More newsmen asking for interviews. The Duke jumped up and called down to Bella, 'Don't answer it. I'm not in.' He ruffled his hair when he caught sight of the mountain of mail and telegrams awaiting his attention. 'I wish I could burn the lot,' he groaned, pushing them aside and letting them scatter on the floor. 'It'll take days and days to answer them. What a waste of time.' He looked longingly at his fiddle. 'I'd sooner start composing some more music.'

'You'll have plenty of time when we get to Sula,' Magnus reminded him.

'So I will!' cried the little Duke, clasping his hands in excitement. 'Christmas in Sula! That'll give me inspiration.' His gaze fell once more on the scattered heap of letters. 'But I doubt if I'll be able to catch the *Hebridean* tomorrow,' he sighed.

'Oh, Duke!' cried Magnus in a disappointed voice.

'Don't worry, boy. I'll come with the next boat.' He gave a boyish grin and added, 'You can run wild for a week, then I'll run wild with you!'

'You'll be sure to come?' said Magnus anxiously.

'Nothing will keep me away!' the Duke assured him.

So that was why Magnus was sailing home alone on the *Hebridean* across the stormy sea to Sula.

A biting north-eastern was whipping up the waves and ruffling the feathers of the seabirds that circled the ship. On the bridge Captain Campbell hunched up his shoulders inside his oilskins and called down, 'It'll be a rough crossing, Magnus. You'd better go down below.'

'I'll bide here,' said Magnus, clinging to the rail.

Stormy or not, he did not want to miss his first sight of Sula. It was like riding a spirited horse as the old ship creaked its way up one wave and down another. Sometimes it lurched drunkenly to one side, then gave a shudder and righted itself. But Magnus enjoyed the movement, planting his feet more firmly on the deck and lurching with the ship.

'What was London like, then?' shouted Captain Campbell.

'It was okay.'

What else could Magnus say? London was not something that could be described in a single sentence. He had not sorted it out in his own mind yet. It was like a kaleidoscope which would have to be shaken about to make a clearer picture. Buckingham Palace, the River Thames, the Tower of London, the galleries filled with paintings by famous artists, the concert hall where he had sat listening to the Duke's music played by a great orchestra. The people.

People! They were everywhere, hurrying along the

crowded streets with anxious looks on their faces as if they had not a moment to lose. The pigeons in Trafalgar Square had looked the most human of the lot. Magnus had already sketched out some rough drawings of them fluttering around the feet of the people who were over-feeding them with handfuls of grain.

'So he's famous now, the wee man,' the captain called down. He was trying to light his pipe, shielding the match inside his oilskin jacket. 'You'll not be seeing so much of him in Sula.'

'I will so!' said Magnus fiercely. 'He's coming with the next boat.' Fame was not going to make any difference to the little Duke.

'They tell me he'll be away to America next. You'll likely be going with him, Magnus.'

'Away!' scoffed Magnus. He had no desire to go to America or anywhere else. Except home to Sula.

There it was! The *Hebridean* took a wide sweep and rounded Sula Point in the teeth of the wind. Little Sula was almost swamped by the waves washing over it. Magnus wondered if any of Gran's black-faced sheep were still there, and if Old Whiskers was hiding in some sheltered nook. It would be great to see the seal again; and, of course, Gran. Even Jinty Cowan. Silly wee thing!

They were all there to meet him when the boat bumped into the pier. The Ferret, Tair, old Cowan, the District Nurse, the minister. The McCallum twins were there, too, tied up in woolly garments like a couple of little dumplings.

Gran stood stiff and straight in the background with the wind whipping her apron up over her face. She held the apron down and looked straight at Magnus. She did not say anything, but her eyes spoke, 'Welcome back, laddie,' and Magnus knew he was home.

Jinty was the first to greet him. Clutching her scarlet tammy to keep it from being whisked off her head, she was hopping like a hen from one foot to another, calling, 'Yoo-hoo, Magnus! I'm here!' She was a daft thing, but for a moment Magnus felt almost fond of her.

Then, as he came down the gangplank, he noticed the strange boy. A pale youth with fair curly hair, dressed in a blue anorak and jeans. He was chittering with cold, hugging himself tight to keep warm.

'It's Lionel. He's Mrs Morrison the minister's wife's nephew. He's come to spend Christmas in Sula with his Auntie,' said Jinty all in the one breath. 'He's *English*, but he's quite nice.'

She gave a giggle and looked through her lashes at the English boy. It was plain that she had found a new admirer, or at least someone new to admire. It should have been a relief to Magnus, yet he felt a trifle huffed when he saw how Jinty gazed at Lionel as if he were one of the wonders of the world.

'How d'you do?' said the boy, holding out his hand.

'Hullo,' said Magnus, but that was as far as he would go. Hand-shakings and how-d'you-do's were not the thing in Sula. He did not like strangers on the island, especially when they were trigged out in fancy anoraks and jeans.

'Lionel's not been well so he's come to stay with his Auntie to get better,' explained Jinty. 'You should hear him singing! Lionel's got an awful good voice. I'm teaching him some Scottish songs. He's going to sing them at the Christmas spree. Aren't you not, Lionel?'

Lionel said little. He shivered in the icy air and hugged himself closer, while Jinty, with two strings to her bow, turned to Magnus and asked, 'How did you get on in London, Magnus?'

'Fine!' said Magnus shortly.

'Lionel lives there so *he's* seen everything. Haven't you, Lionel?' She smiled at the English boy and then turned back to Magnus. 'Did you see the Royal Family?' she wanted to know. But Magnus had escaped from her clutches, with Rory the collie dog bounding at his heels. He wanted to be alone to savour the feeling of Sula, to take great gulps of sea air and to rush up to the top of the Heathery Hill.

Later he would seek out the Hermit, fight with the Ferret, ride Sheltie the pony, and search for Old Whiskers. But now it was enough just to be here, with the snell wind blowing the seagulls off course and bending the stunted rowan in the Manse garden. Never mind Lionel; never mind London. Nothing on earth could compare with the joy of being back on his own island.

Next day the storm started.

'Mag-nus!' called Gran. 'It's going to snow.'

Gran was never wrong. Better than any barometer, she could sense in which direction the wind would blow, and warn the men when to keep their fishing boats in the harbour. Many a life she had saved through her wise forecasting. But not her son's. Magnus's father had been lost in a sudden squall off Sula Point and his mother had died soon after of a broken heart. Since then Gran had been even more anxious to recognize warning signs from the sky.

Almost as soon as she spoke the snow began to fall. Great feathery flakes fluttered down, settling on the hedges and dykes like a sprinkling of sugar. Snow seldom lay long on the island, melting the moment it reached the ground. But this was different. There had been a hard frost during the night and the flakes remained where they fell, waiting for more to pile on top of them.

Like Gran, the animals had sensed the oncoming of the storm. The sheep had wandered down from the Heathery Hill and were cowering behind the stone dykes for protection. The cocks and hens gathered in uneasy groups, cackling to each other as if holding a committee meeting. Then one by one they straggled away to seek shelter in the hen-houses. Sheltie, of his own accord, trotted into the old shed behind Gran's cottage, and the seabirds huddled on the cliffs, crying like children.

'Mag-nus!' Gran came stamping out of the house with a pail in her hand and an old sack flung over her shoulders. 'You'd better go across to Little Sula and fetch the sheep. There are still two left there.'

'Okay, Gran.'

'Get somebody to help.'

Gran would have gone herself if she had not had so many urgent jobs to do. The beasts to feed, the cow to milk, the peat to bring in before the storm grew worse.

Jinty was hovering in the Cowans' doorway, looking like a snow-maiden with the white flakes gathering on her scarlet tammy and covering her shoulders like a mantle. She was at a loose end. Lionel had caught a chill and was sitting sneezing by the Manse fireside. So now she could turn all her attention to Magnus. Her first love.

'Let me come, Magnus. I'll help you.'

But Magnus was not wanting a lassie to help him. 'I'll get the Ferret,' he said gruffly.

The Ferret was willing enough, though he pretended not to be. He and Magnus seldom said a civil word to each other, yet the feeling was there deep down.

As they rowed across the stormy stretch of water to Little Sula, the Ferret suddenly said, 'What do you think of him?'

'Him?'

'Thon chap from London. Lionel! What a name!'

'What's wrong with him?' asked Magnus. He had the same feeling himself, though he was not going to let the Ferret know.

'Och, nothing,' said the Ferret. Nothing he could lay his finger on. Yet there was something. 'He's a softie!'

There was nothing soft about the Ferret. He would row on till his arms dropped off and never complain about being cold or exhausted. Though he was smaller than Magnus he was as tough as a tyke, and the two matched each other in strength and stubbornness. They would fight to the finish, leaving each other with black eyes and bloody noses; yet, win or lose, feeling no bitterness in the end.

Magnus forgot about Lionel and everything else when he suddenly saw a seal nosing its way up to the surface.

'Whiskers!' he cried, leaning out of the boat so that he could pat the seal on the snout. 'It's great to see you!'

Old Whiskers gave a grunt of satisfaction. The boy was home and all was well.

2 The Snowman

Gran's two black-faced sheep were standing solemnly on the shore of Little Sula like passengers waiting to be picked up. No need to chase after them or coax them into the boat. The little island was already white with snow and the sheep shivering with cold.

'Come on, then!' said the Ferret, using all his wiry strength to heave them into the boat. He had to blink away the snowflakes freezing on his eyelashes. 'Get in!'

It was harder rowing back against the wind with the heavy load and the snow blowing horizontally against the boys' faces. Magnus and the Ferret had to tug at the oars with all their might to keep on course. There was no time for words, not that the two had much to say to each other at any time. But at least they were pulling together for a change.

Magnus felt a surge of excitement as he looked ahead and saw how Sula had been transformed under its covering of snow. The Manse rowan looked like a Christmas tree, the Heathery Hill was a sugar-loaf and the shabby cottages were little snow-white palaces. What a picture he could draw! His heart beat faster at the prospect of the holidays ahead. It was going to be a real Christmas in Sula. The first time they had ever had a snowstorm.

His spirits took a sudden downward plunge when the Ferret said, 'If the storm goes on, the boat'll not get across.'

'What boat?'

'The *Hebridean*,' said the Ferret. 'The wee Duke'll not get here for Christmas.'

'It looks just like His Grace,' said Jinty Cowan. And for once she was right.

Magnus stared at the snowman he had been building: the first he had ever made. There had never been enough snow in Sula before for such ploys. Now there was too much.

It lay in mounds all over the island, blown into fantastic shapes by the wind. Where was the church? A high pyramid of pure white stood in its place. Every hedge and ditch was filled to overflowing, and the Heathery Hill looked twice its size, merging with the snow-clouds in the sky. The edges of the sea were frozen over, and the boats locked in a tight grip of ice, with the seabirds skittering across it like amateur skaters. Icicles as strong as stalactites hung down from the roofs and doorways, and the whole island looked as if it had been drenched in whipped cream.

For hours Magnus had been absorbed in his task, but with a niggling worry at the back of his mind. Was that why the snowman had taken on the appearance of the little Duke? Magnus had been thinking of him all the time he was heaping up the snow and moulding it into the form of a man. In a way, it was like painting a picture. He had copied the features, wrinkles and all, and even tried to fashion the fluted edges of a kilt around the snowman's body.

'It's not bad,' he thought, standing back to study his efforts with a certain amount of satisfaction. But Magnus would sooner have seen the Duke in the flesh. He was still hoping against hope that the boat might get through, if the storm broke in time.

A snowball came whizzing past his head, fired by the Ferret. A near miss.

'Watch it, you!' warned Magnus and scooped up a handful of snow, ready to fire back.

The Ferret was in his element, with plenty of ammunition at his command. This was better than his catapult. He had made a pile of hard round snowballs and was looking for targets to bombard. A wicked gleam came into his eye when he saw the boy Lionel making his way towards them, in borrowed wellingtons and with the minister's woolly scarf wound round his neck.

The London boy was still looking pale and peaky, but boredom had driven him from the Manse fire, and he was eager for some human contact of his own generation.

'I say, that's jolly good,' he said to Magnus, blowing on his gloved hands and staring admiringly at the snowman. 'May I help?'

'No,' said Magnus, briefly and bluntly. He was putting the finishing touches to the Duke's sporran and was needing neither praise nor help from anyone, least of all from such a namby-pamby creature as Lionel. He was aware at the back of his mind that he was being selfish. At the High School in Cronan he was learning a little about the rules of give and take, but found it difficult to put them into practice.

Lionel looked deflated. He jumped from one foot to the other to keep his circulation going, then looked hopefully at the Ferret, but there was no sign of friendship there. He was too late to duck when the first snowball came flying through the air. It caught him on the nose, and before he had time to recover, the bombardment began in earnest. Volley after volley.

'I say!' he protested, putting up his hands to protect his

21

face; but it was too late. Soon his eyes were blinded, his mouth was full of snow, and his face smarting from the stinging blows. He made a feeble effort to hit back, but the Ferret had the advantage with so many ready-made snowballs to fire off.

Magnus looked on, remaining neutral for a time. Then his sense of justice came to the surface.

'Stop that!' he shouted at the Ferret.

'I will not!' said the Ferret defiantly. 'Who'll stop me?'

'Me!" said Magnus, getting ready for action.

Lionel took cover behind the snowman while the battle raged. He seemed appalled at its ferocity, though it was only an everyday fight between two well-matched sparring partners; one of a hundred they had fought without thinking anything of it.

The Ferret's ammunition flew thick and fast, with Magnus bearing the brunt as he stooped down to scoop up handfuls of snow. Then suddenly he changed his tactics and rushed the Ferret off his feet. Down fell the pair of them, rolling over and over in the snow, locked in deadly combat.

'Oh, I say! You'll hurt yourselves,' cried Lionel, peering out from behind the snowman. 'Do stop!'

Magnus and the Ferret paid no attention to his advice. It was one of their best battles. They punched and pummelled, they stuffed each other's faces in the snow, they groaned and grunted like a couple of wild animals. It was great!

Finally, through sheer exhaustion, they gave up and sat back to back, covered from head to foot in snow. Both felt a sense of relief at having given vent to their animal spirits. They would fight again when the occasion arose, but now they were content to call a truce.

Jinty came skidding out of the Cowans' cottage, which was also the General Store and Post Office. She was muffled to the eyebrows against the cold, and had an important look on her face as if she had some special news to impart. Little Miss Know-All liked nothing better.

'We're cut off! The telephone's broken down!' She paused, like a seasoned actress, to let the news sink in before delivering her next lines. 'We can't get in touch with the mainland. If the storm goes on, we'll maybe starve to death.'

It was nonsense of course. In Sula there were ways and means of surviving. The islanders could live on their humps for months. Plenty of meal and flour, hams hanging from every ceiling, sheep and hens to be killed if the necessity arose. It was the extras they would miss. The treats brought in by the *Hebridean* each week. Sausages, kippers, and fruit. There would be no newspapers or letters, no word at all from the outside world.

Worst of all for Magnus, he would not be able to ring up Cronan Castle and get in touch with the Duke.

He got up and dusted the snow off his body. He was not going to show his feelings in front of the others. He tightened his lips and set to work once more on the snowman, putting in extra touches to the Duke's face with more care than before.

'Thanks, Magnus,' said Lionel, coming forward and laying a hand on his arm.

'What for?' asked Magnus gruffly, shaking off the hand.

'For taking my part against him,' said Lionel, indicating the Ferret. 'It was jolly good of you, Magnus.'

'Away!' said Magnus, embarrassed and angry.

He had enjoyed fighting the Ferret and was not wanting any thanks for it. The London boy looked at him with a puzzled expression, and was about to say something more when Jinty came darting forward, like an anxious hen rounding up her chick.

'Lionel! You shouldn't be standing out here in the cold. Come into our house and get warm. Poor soul! You're perishing.'

Lionel looked as if he would sooner have perished, but his will was not strong enough to resist Jinty's. Magnus had a faint feeling of pity for him as he meekly followed her away, thinking of the over-heated house with its clutter of cushions and ornaments. But the Ferret had no such feelings.

'Sissy!' he shouted, and flung another snowball at Lionel's back.

Mrs Gillies, the District Nurse, came tramping through the snow in a pair of big boots, carrying her black bag. No hope of riding her bicycle in such weather. There was a worried note in her voice as she called out, 'You'd better not get ill, any of you. We'll get no help from the mainland, so watch it. I'm away to take the McCallum twins' temperatures. They're looking a bit off-colour.'

The Ferret aimed a snowball at her and then thought the better of it. He would be no match for Mrs Gillies if she got her dander up. All the same, she was looking a bit off-colour herself. Normally she would have been elated at the prospect of the islanders falling ill, for the District Nurse liked being fully-stretched, as she called it, and could never have enough patients to satisfy her.

The truth was, Mrs Gillies was sickening for something herself, and by the end of the day was forced to take to her bed.

'It's only a cold,' she said crossly, when Gran called at her cottage with soup and other comforts. 'Give me a day and I'll be as right as rain.'

But Gran knew better. Magnus had come with the old woman, carrying a lantern to light her on her way. Now he was standing near the door, not knowing what to do with himself. It was strange seeing Mrs Gillies in bed, wearing a flannel nightgown, with her hair in an untidy grey pigtail, behaving like a fractious child.

'What'll everybody do without me?' she whined.

'We'll get on fine,' said Gran firmly. 'Lie still. You've got a temperature.' And, indeed Mrs Gillies' face was flushed, though she was shivering under the bedclothes. 'Put on the kettle,' Gran said sharply to Magnus. 'She'll need more hot-water bottles. You'd better go back home and bring another.'

Magnus went thankfully out into the freezing night.

The sky was a pale milky-white. Even the few stars that were visible seemed to be shivering with cold. Everything was uncannily still. No sound of lapping water, no bird-calls, not a whirr of a wing. The crunching of the ice beneath his feet was the only sound to be heard.

The snowman stood stiff and straight, like a marble statue of the Duke. It had a permanent look about it as if it would never melt. Indeed the whole island seemed locked for ever in an icy grip.

As Magnus passed along the row of houses near the harbour he heard a hideous noise coming from the Ferret's cottage. Like a lost soul wailing in torment. It was the Ferret playing the bagpipes. The red-haired laddie was no musician, it was only something to do to while away the time. Magnus mentally closed his ears and hurried by, then shuddered again when he heard *The Blue Danube* blaring out from the Cowans' wheezy gramophone.

He tried to recapture the lovely strains of the *Sula Symphony* which he had listened to, entranced, in the concert hall in London. He had not known that there were so many varied instruments in an orchestra, nor that they could all merge together into such a harmonious whole. It was exciting to watch how the conductor gathered them all under the beat of his baton; even more wonderful to hear.

The music conjured up such vivid pictures of Sula that Magnus had felt he was not there, in the thronged hall, but home on his own island. In the end, he was not seeing the 'cellos and the fiddles, but Little Sula, the Heathery Hill and the Merry Dancers flashing across the night sky.

The little Duke sat by his side, with his head buried in his hands as if he was ashamed of himself. But he was listening intently to every note. Now and again he dug

Magnus in the ribs and said in an excited whisper, 'That's it, boy! They've got it!'

Magnus knew most of the music already, but not put together and played like this. The Duke had gone over and over it in the Tower room, polishing each phrase as Mr Skinnymalink polished the stones of Sula. Now the great crashing sounds reminded him of the sea pounding against the rocks, and the gentler passages of a lark singing its heart out in the sunny sky.

The audience sat silent, as if under a spell. At the end, when the applause broke out, Magnus had felt hot tears smarting in his eyes and there was a lump in his throat. He wanted to convey his feelings to the Duke, but all he could gulp was, 'It's great!' There were plenty of others to praise the little man, but Magnus's approval meant more to him.

'You're the one who inspired me, boy,' he said, with a glint of tears in his own eyes. 'You and Sula.'

But there was little inspiration in the tinny tunes coming from the Cowans' creaky gramophone. Magnus hurried past their door and into Gran's cottage, glad to see the glow from the peat fire. Specky the hen was sitting drowsing on the rug like a cat, with the boiling kettle spitting out at her. Magnus swung it to the side, said, 'Hullo, you!' to Specky and went to fetch the stone hot-water bottle to take to Mrs Gillies.

In his bedroom he found his drawing book, full of the rough sketches he had made in London. He hesitated for a moment, then picked it up and took it downstairs. He was itching to add some snow scenes to the book while they were still fresh in his mind.

He squatted down on the rug beside the hen. Gran would be waiting for him, but he would indulge himself for only a few minutes. He did not notice the time as it ticked away from Gran's old wag-at-the wa'. A quarter of an hour ... Half an hour ...

He had roughed out the snowman and drawn a gull losing its balance as it skated dizzily across the ice. Now he was copying the frosty pictures on the window pane. They were so cleverly woven together that they might have been fashioned by a designer instead of by Jack Frost.

Magnus was so absorbed that at first he did not hear the thumping at the door. When it came again he started guiltily to his feet.

'What is it?' he called, and hurried to open the door.

It was Lionel, the London boy, who came stumbling in, white as a sheet, his eyes staring like those of a frightened animal.

'What's up?' asked Magnus in alarm.

Lionel had no breath left to put words into a sentence. But what he said was enough to confirm Magnus's fears.

'The Manse! It's on fire! Come!'

3 Fire and Fear

Magnus dashed out of the door and saw that the blaze
from the Manse was lighting up the island like a great
bonfire, brighter than the Northern Lights. Flames
streaked across the sky, sparks danced in the air like small
stars. It was a sight both fascinating and frightening.
Never before had there been such a fire in Sula.

'Fire!'

Magnus thumped on every door and called out the
warning as he ran past. There was no fire brigade on the
island, and every hand was needed to help. The boy had a
guilty feeling that it had all been his fault. If he had not
sat so long on the rug indulging himself with his
sketching, he might have seen the start of the fire and
done something to arrest it.

Lionel stumbled after him, trying to tell how it had
happened, but Magnus hardly heard him. All he could
think of was whether the minister and his wife were safe.

'Are they all right?' he shouted to Lionel.

'Yes, but Auntie's worried about the cat. Blackie's due
to have kittens . . .'

Magnus had better things to think about than Blackie.
Getting to the blazing Manse as quickly as possible was
his first objective. It was not easy, slipping and sliding
over the snow in the darkness. He heard shouts behind
him and was relieved to know that the others were
following. Old Cowan, McCallum, and every able-bodied
man and woman on the island were hurrying to the rescue.

The Reverend Alexander Morrison was standing

amongst the snow wreaths in the Manse garden, wringing his hands helplessly.

'Isn't it terrible!' he groaned. 'What can we do to stop it? All the pipes are frozen.' So how could they quench the flames without water?

Old Cowan had arrived on the scene and was taking command. 'Fetch pails!' he shouted. 'We'll have to use the snow.'

The men hurried off to find pails and buckets, while Magnus scooped up great handfuls of snow to fling on the flames. It was little enough help, but soon everyone was doing the same, even the minister, who stopped moaning now that he had something useful to do.

The Ferret was in his element with a real target to snowball, and none worked harder. He scooped and flung, scooped and flung, long after his arms ached beyond endurance. Lionel, too, did his best, though he was soon gasping with exhaustion; but at least their combined efforts were helping to keep the fire from spreading further.

It had started in the minister's study. 'I was sitting in the easy chair smoking my pipe,' he told anyone who would listen. 'I must have dozed off and the pipe fell on to the carpet. The next thing I knew . . .'

'Where's Mrs Morrison?' asked Magnus stopping his work to look around at the little group of helpers. He could see Mr Skinnymalink filling a bucket with snow, and the schoolmaster limping backwards and forwards, working as hard as any. Even Jinty had come, and for once was not thinking of herself in her eagerness to be of use. Old Cowan had organized them into a line, so that they could pass their pails and buckets from one hand to another, but the minister's wife was not amongst them.

'Good gracious! She must have gone inside to look for the cat,' said the minister, starting forward. But Magnus pushed him back and said, 'Stay there, Mr Morrison. I'll go.'

He stepped into the smoke-filled house, shouting : 'Mrs Morrison! Are you there?' His eyes smarted and the smoke stung his throat as he forced his way forward. Then to his relief he saw a shadowy figure groping about in front of him and heard Mrs Morrison calling in a hysterical voice, 'Blackie! Where are you, Blackie?'

She was half-fainting when Magnus reached her side. He caught her by the arm and tried to urge her back towards the open door. 'Come outside,' he said urgently. 'It's not safe in here.'

'I can't come without Blackie. She's expecting her kittens . . .'

'I'll find her. Come on, Mrs Morrison,' said Magnus firmly, and half-dragged her out into the cold air. He knew it would be foolish to go back in again, but he had given his word. So, ignoring old Cowan's cries of, 'Come back, Magnus,' he forced his way once more into the burning house.

Magnus could see little except smoke; then suddenly he was aware that he was not alone. Lionel had followed him in, coughing and gasping as the acrid smoke caught at his throat. 'The kitchen,' he said in a strangled voice. 'I think Blackie's there. In a basket.'

He was overcome by another fit of coughing, and Magnus took hold of him and pushed him towards the door. If the cat was to be saved he would do it on his own. Lionel would be more hindrance than help, no matter how good his intentions might be.

The only way he could reach the cat without being overcome by smoke and flames was to get down on his hands and knees and crawl. He could hear a faint miaowing and see the scorched basket where Blackie was lying.

'Come on, puss,' he called, trying to urge her to jump out, but the cat would not move. Then suddenly Magnus knew why. Blackie was not alone in the basket. She was purring with a mixture of pride and anxiety over her newly-born kittens.

Magnus's head was reeling and he was half-choked with smoke as he took a sudden dive forward and grabbed the basket. Then he fled back along the passage and out into the safety of the snow-filled garden.

'Here!' he said, taking a gulp of cold air and dumping the basket at Mrs Morrison's feet. 'She's had five kittens and they're okay.'

Magnus would never forget the strangeness of that scene in the Manse garden. The people silhouetted against the snow, the flames leaping up towards the night sky, the smoke billowing out into fantastic shapes.

There were few words spoken. Everyone worked silently and desperately. Bucket after bucket of snow passed from one helping hand to another and was emptied on to the flames till at last they began to flicker and die out. The blaze was conquered.

The people stood back, their faces black and their arms aching. There was little they could do now. Except give shelter to the homeless.

'Come and stay in the schoolhouse,' said Andrew Murray, limping towards the minister and his wife. 'There's room for you both. The kittens, too!'

Mrs Morrison was clutching the basket as if it was her most prized possession. 'What about Lionel?' she asked anxiously. Her nephew was looking in worse shape than any of them.

'I'll take him in,' said Gran, striding forward. 'He can have Magnus's room.'

'Oh, Gran!'

With the crisis over, all Magnus wanted was to creep home to the peace and privacy of his own small bedroom. He thought of his few treasured possessions and his jealously-guarded paintings. But Gran gave him a quick hard look that brought him to his senses. This was no time for selfish feelings, with Lionel on the point of collapse.

'Let's go home,' he said, taking hold of Lionel's arm. 'You take the other side,' he told the Ferret sharply.

The Ferret made a face but did as he was bid, and together they half-carried Lionel across the snow towards the houses at the harbour. Jinty, slithering behind them and gasping for breath in the cold air, could still find her tongue. 'What about you, Magnus? Come and sleep in our house.'

'He'll sleep in the press,' said Gran bluntly. 'Go home and mind your own business, Jinty Cowan. You'd better watch yourself, with the District Nurse ill.'

'Is she awful ill?' asked Jinty, scenting more drama.

'She'll pull through,' said Gran shortly. 'She's sleeping.'

Magnus thought guiltily of the hot-water bottle he had never taken to Mrs Gillies. The first thing Gran did when they got home was to fill it for Lionel. 'See him up to bed,' she told Magnus. 'He looks all in.'

Magnus went up the creaking stairs, lighting the way with the little lamp he used at night. He tried not to feel resentful when he saw Lionel's head lying on his pillow. The boy's face was almost as white as the pillow itself, as if all the blood had been drained out of him.

'Are you all right?' asked Magnus uneasily.

Lionel turned his head and looked at him, but he was too weak to speak. He gave a nod, then closed his eyes and turned his head away.

'You'd better have a hot drink,' said Gran when Magnus went down into the lamplit kitchen. Specky was still on the rug, and he sat down beside her, drinking the mug of hot milk. Both he and Gran were too weary to speak.

Presently she rose and fetched some blankets and an old eiderdown. 'There! Away you go to the press, laddie, and get some sleep.'

It was not often Gran called him laddie. It brought a warm feeling to Magnus's heart as he lay huddled under the bedclothes in the dark press where his dead father's oilskins hung on a hook on the wall. It was little more than a cupboard, dark and airless, but Magnus was too tired to care. In a moment he had floated off into a dreamless sleep and all the cares of the day were forgotten.

It was a few days before the snow stopped falling, but Sula was still imprisoned in an icy grip.

Magnus wondered if he would ever see the black earth again and the wild flowers growing. Where was Old Whiskers? Every creepy-crawly creature had vanished underground as if they had never existed. The seabirds could sometimes be heard making piteous cries as they flew around, trying to find food and refuge. Every nook, cranny and cave was crowded. The birds huddled there like displaced persons, pecking dejectedly at their feathers. The uneasy stillness on the island gave everyone a lost feeling.

The Duke, standing still and straight in the snow, seemed to be watching over everything. Until he began to melt there was little hope of life returning to normal. Old Cowan and the other men made a brave attempt at patching up the Manse, tearing out half-burned beams and clearing up the rubble of broken glass, but they were sadly hampered by the bitter cold. Every now and then they had to stop and nurse their frozen fingers back to life.

Magnus had burns on his legs which stung in the cold air, and Jinty's hands were blotched with chilblains; but these were minor ills which the District Nurse could have cured if she had been on her feet. She had taken the turn, Gran thought. Now it was the boy Lionel who was most in need of nursing.

He tossed and turned in Magnus's narrow bed, murmuring in his troubled sleep. When he was awake he made no demands, but lay quietly trying to stifle his fits of coughing and looking gratefully at Magnus when Gran sent him up with a refilled bottle or a hot drink.

Magnus felt uneasy, not knowing what to say to him. It was strange having such an alien presence in his room, changing its personality in some subtle way. Yet, as the days went by, it was not so much the intrusion on his privacy that troubled him, as a genuine concern for the sick boy. Lionel's helplessness touched something in Magnus's heart, like the feeling he had for a wounded animal who could not take care of himself. He watched anxiously every sup of soup the invalid took, and tried to press him to swallow another mouthful.

'Go on, it'll do you good. Are you feeling any better?'

Lionel nodded his head, but he was still too weak to speak. Every time Magnus left the room his heart was heavy with worry. When the Ferret, busy with his snowballs, called out, 'How's that namby-pamby Lionel?' Magnus felt his hackles rising and shouted back, 'Shut up, you!' to the Ferret's surprise. And to his own. Strange that he should feel protective towards someone he had disliked so fiercely at first sight.

But everything was strange. Magnus had a feeling of

being in limbo, waiting for something to happen. Christmas was coming nearer, but only Tair believed that Santa Claus would come, though Magnus would sooner have seen the *Hebridean* sailing into the harbour with the little Duke on board.

It was Avizandum who had told Tair that Santa was on his way.

'That's great,' said Tair, who believed everything the invisible little creature in his pocket told him. 'Will he be bringing presents?'

'Of course.'

'What will mine be?'

'Depends what you asked for,' said Avizandum cautiously. 'Did you shout up the chimney?'

'Yes, I did. I asked for a gun. Is that what I'm getting?'

But Avizandum knew when to vanish! It was not so often nowadays that his presence was felt. He seemed to be jealous of the twins, who took up so much of Tair's attention. They were now beginning to totter about and to speak in a mixed-up kind of way. Tair took his duties as elder brother seriously, and was for ever helping them over hurdles, teaching them new words and picking them up when they tumbled. He himself had grown bigger and sturdier and was now wearing Magnus's cast-off Harris tweed suit. But in moments of stress he still looked in his pocket to see if his old friend was there.

'Avizandum!'

'What?'

'How will Santa Claus get here?'

'Through the air, of course.'

'But, how . . .?'

'Good-bye!' said Avizandum hurriedly. The twins had appeared at the door, bundled up in their woolly trappings, and were toddling towards Tair. He could get nothing more out of Avizandum; but if *he* had said Santa would come, he would come.

The rest of the islanders took a more practical view. If there were any presents to be given they would have to make them themselves from the few materials available. In every household there were small secret gifts hidden away, ready to be handed out on Christmas Day.

Gran had knitted a pair of warm gloves for Magnus and saved up enough sugar to make treacle toffee for the twins. Jinty was trying to crochet a multi-coloured hat from bits of leftover wool. For Magnus or Lionel? She was not sure yet. It would look better on Lionel's fair head, and Magnus never wore a hat if he could avoid it; but what could she give *him*? A handkerchief, perhaps, with a large M sewn in coloured thread in one corner.

Mr Skinnymalink, the Hermit, had found a new skill. Unable to collect and polish the stones of Sula, hidden deep under the snow, he had turned his attention to wood. In the schoolhouse shed he had picked up a small chunk of hazel wood and started whittling at it with his knife. Suddenly, to his satisfaction, he found he had a facility for shaping and moulding it into a figure. Each day he grew more absorbed as he made small wooden toys for the island children: animals and birds, dolls for the twins, and for Magnus a seal that looked like Old Whiskers.

The present Magnus would have liked best was a link with Cronan Castle. Day after day the telephone remained silent, and all hope of the little Duke coming to Sula was gone.

Then suddenly, when he least expected it, the miracle happened.

4 A Surprise Visitor

The McCallum twins were missing.

Their mother came calling at each house asking if anyone had seen them. Like Specky the hen, Rose and Angus had a habit of wandering in at any open door. The twins were communal children, welcome in every household. But in the grip of the snowstorm all doors were kept closed, and no one had seen the toddlers coming or going.

Where could they be? Surely they could not have strayed far amongst the great mounds of snow that lay around the houses at the harbour. It was difficult enough for grown-ups to keep from falling, and the twins were not yet used to walking any distance on their own. The fear that they might have roamed towards the sea edge and fallen through the ice was uppermost in everyone's minds.

Tair was frantic with worry. He ran here and there calling the children's names. Calling, too, for Avizandum to come to his aid. But in Tair's hour of need the little fellow in his pocket had deserted him. Anything to do with the twins sent him into a jealous huff.

The searchers spread out all over the island, trying to find traces of the missing children, but the surface was frozen so hard that there were no footprints to be seen. If the twins had wandered as far as the Heathery Hill, they could have slipped and tumbled into a snow-filled ditch. If so, they must surely have perished in the bitter cold. The very thought brought a feeling of dread to Magnus's heart.

'Rory!' he called to the collie. 'Come on, boy. Help me to look.'

But in which direction should they go? The dog was as unsure as the boy. Rory sniffed the ground and recoiled when the snow stung at his nostrils. There was no familiar scent to be picked up. He gave an unhappy yowl and slunk back at Magnus's heels.

Suddenly they came upon Tair wandering round in circles, tears trickling down his cheeks. They were already beginning to freeze on his face and he looked so desolate that Magnus took him by the hand. 'Go home and stay by the fire, Tair. You'll get frozen out here.'

'No!' Tair pushed Magnus away. 'I'm not going home without the twins.' He gulped back a sob and said, 'I wish Avizandum would help. He always knows everything.' He put his hand in his pocket and pleaded, 'Come on, Avizandum. Tell me.'

Magnus had enough sense not to ridicule him. He knew how dependent Tair was on the invisible creature in his pocket. Avizandum was more real to the small boy than any of the flesh-and-blood people in Sula.

'Wheesht!' said Tair suddenly.

He had felt a stirring in his pocket and heard a faint whisper. 'What is it, Avizandum? Are you going to tell me something about the twins?'

'Them!' he heard the little creature say grumpily. 'They can stay where they are.'

'Where?' asked Tair eagerly.

'I'm not telling!'

'Please, Avizandum,' pleaded Tair, with a break in his voice.

There was silence for a moment, then a faint whisper. 'Beside the pig—'

'The pig?' Tair looked puzzled. Did Avizandum mean

40

a real pig or a stone hot-water bottle?

Avizandum was gone, but Magnus was suddenly on the alert.

'Porky!' he cried out. Old Cowan's pig. Perhaps the twins had wandered into the pigsty and been shut in there. 'Come on, Rory.'

Rory was already bounding away towards the pigsty, sniffing at the door and barking with excitement.

'You see!' cried Tair, wiping away his frozen tears. 'Avizandum's never wrong.'

The twins were lying asleep on the straw at the side of the pig's trough, with Porky keeping guard over them. He seemed content enough to have their company and began grumphing angrily when the door opened and Magnus let in a blast of icy air.

'Here they are! They're safe.' He called out to Tair.
'Run and tell your mother.'

Tair jumped up and down with joy. Then he tore off
like a whirlwind to spread the good news. Soon the twins
were carried safely home, none the worse for their outing.

And now Tair had become involved in another drama.
The small voice could be heard speaking to him in an
excited voice.

'Speak up, Avizandum.'

'Santa Claus is coming.'

'So he is!' Tair stared up into the sky. 'Look, Magnus!
He's flying in. On a big bird.'

It was the biggest bird ever seen hovering over Sula.
Magnus called out, 'It's a helicopter. Mercy me! It's
coming down. I wonder! Could it be ...?'

It was!

The helicopter hung overhead as if suspended from the
sky. Then slowly and carefully it made its approach. The
flattest surface was the snow-covered field behind the
Cowans' cottage. All the people who had rushed out to
watch held their breath as the big bird wheeled and
turned, then dropped down and settled with a shudder on
the snow.

The door opened, and out came a strange figure
wearing a moth-eaten fur coat which reached down to the
ground. He had a pair of goggles over his eyes, a balaclava
helmet on his head, and a large sack slung over his
shoulder.

'Is that Santa Claus?' asked Tair in a puzzled voice.

'It's the Duke!' cried Magnus, rushing towards him.

The little man pushed back his goggles and grinned
with delight. 'You didn't think I was going to miss
Christmas in Sula, did you? No fear!' He gripped the boy
by the hand, and suddenly the sun shone out.

'Oh, Duke! It's great to see you.'

'Great to see you, boy. Come along; help me to unload the stuff.'

The pilot and navigator handed out parcels and crates containing food and presents for the islanders, with Magnus and the Ferret acting as willing helpers. Then, after a few words to the crew, the Duke stepped back. The great bird began to shudder and shake before gathering itself together and whirring away upwards into the sky. The next moment it had flown away over Little Sula, looking as small as a seagull.

Now that the little Duke was here, nothing mattered to Magnus. It was as if everything had suddenly begun to stir to life once more. The little man himself was as excited as a schoolboy, talking and laughing, prancing about from one foot to the other.

'Bless my soul!' he cried, clapping his hands when he caught sight of his snow-image. 'So that's what I look like!' He turned to Magnus. 'You did it, boy. I know you did.' He went forward to examine the snowman more closely. 'It's a work of art! I wish I could take it home with me to Cronan Castle. But, mark my word, it'll melt before long.' He sniffed the air. 'D'you know what, boy? The thaw is coming.'

The Duke was right. Not only had he brought good cheer to the island, for the first time in weeks the snow-clouds lightened and the sun came shining through, lifting the load from everyone's shoulders. Spirits rose at the prospect of the long siege coming to an end.

There was one big problem. Where was His Grace going to sleep? Like the twins, he would have been content to share Porky's sty, but it was hardly the place for a blue-blooded Duke. In normal times he would have gone to the schoolhouse or the Manse, and Magnus would willingly have given up his own bed if it had not already been occupied by the ailing Lionel.

It was Gran as usual who solved the problem. 'I'll put clean sheets on the box-bed in the kitchen and he can sleep there.'

Magnus's heart gave a bound of joy. It would be wonderful being under the same roof as the little Duke. But what about Gran who normally slept in the box-bed?

'I'll sleep at Mrs Gillies's,' she said briskly. 'Magnus, bring Himself home. He'll be ready for a hot cup of tea.'

Himself was delighted with the arrangements. Later that night he and Magnus sat together in the lamplit kitchen eating their supper. Gran had gone, and at last they could have a heart-to-heart talk. The peat fire was burning brightly, there were fresh sheets on the box-bed and a hot pig tucked inside it. What more could the Duke want?

Nothing.

'This is the life, boy,' he said, beaming with pleasure as he looked around him at the peaceful scene: the plain furniture, the well-scrubbed floor, the one picture on the wall, the kettle spitting on the swey, and Specky asleep on the rug with her head tucked under her feathers.

'It's years since I slept in a box-bed. Years and years!' (The truth was, he had never slept in one in his life.) 'I'm going to enjoy my dreams tonight.'

'Eat your supper,' said Magnus, as if speaking to a child.

The supper was as plain as the kitchen but the Duke did justice to it, relishing every mouthful of Gran's home-made bannocks and oatcakes. She had boiled an egg for him, one of the few Specky had laid during the storm, and as he picked up the horn egg-spoon he looked at Magnus and said, 'Are you not having one, too, boy?'

'I'll just have some cheese,' said Magnus hastily.

There was little enough of that left. Indeed, all supplies were running short. The best Gran could provide had been given to the invalid upstairs to tempt his appetite, and Magnus had to be content with anything that was left over. Not that he minded. The Duke was here, the thaw was coming, and he had nothing left to wish for.

'Here! You take half, boy,' said the Duke, dissecting the egg with a quick thrust of the horn spoon. 'Let's share it. And pour me out another cup of tea. It's the best I've tasted.'

Magnus fetched the big brown teapot from the hob and filled the Duke's cup, thinking what a wonderful companion he was, finding enjoyment in the simplest things. Even drinking a cup of Gran's well-brewed tea. As they shared the egg, the Duke said, 'Now then, boy; tell me everything.'

It was only in the Duke's company that Magnus could loosen his tongue. Even so, he never found it easy to put his thoughts into words. It would have been simpler for him to make pictures of everything that had happened. The oncome of the storm, the fire at the Manse, the District Nurse's illness, the twins lying asleep in Porky's sty, and Lionel tossing and turning in the bed upstairs.

Magnus did his best with his halting vocabulary, while the Duke listened intently. At the end the little man cried out, 'Bless my soul! There's always something happening in Sula. Thank goodness I came. Which reminds me, I brought something with me. Something special.'

Everything the Duke had brought was special. After the monotony of their diet, the sight of a crate of oranges was enough to make the islanders lick their lips. There had been enough to share around with everyone. Packages and bundles were still piled high in the hallway – the

45

lobby, Gran called it – containing more festive fare for everyone to enjoy.

'Let's unpack them,' said the Duke when they had finished their supper. 'I want to find you own special parcel.'

He handed it to the boy and, simmering with excitement, said, 'Go on, open it. Don't bother about the knots. Cut the string.'

Magnus took out his pocket knife and for once ignored Gran's waste-not-want-not teachings. He cut through the string, tore off the paper and found a book inside. No ordinary book. There was something familiar about the picture on the cover.

Surely that was the Heathery Hill in the background, with the houses at the harbour and the *Hebridean* lumbering her way towards the pier. Puffins and cormorants, gulls and gannets flew in and out of the design, and the seal that lay on the rock could only be Old Whiskers.

'It's yours, boy, yours! Read what it says on the cover.' The little Duke thrust the book closer to Magnus and read out the words himself. '*The Story of Sula*, by Andrew Murray. Illustrated by Magnus Macduff. That's you, boy. Magnus Macduff, artist.'

Magnus felt his face flushing. His heart raced faster as he turned the pages and saw his own work reproduced throughout the book. Some were full-page drawings of island scenes: the sheep being sheared, Gran gathering peat, the fishing boats rounding Sula Point, the lifeboat being launched.

Others were vignettes, like the ones he drew round the margins of his lesson books. Crabs, jellyfish, Sheltie the pony, Rory, the rowan tree, the Fairy Ring on Little Sula. And always more seals and seabirds. The whole of Sula was there, captured in words and pictures. But it was the pictures that brought the book to life.

'They're not bad,' thought Magnus with a stab of pride.

But he could do better. He must do better. Since he had seen the paintings in the great galleries in London he knew how much there was still to learn. The sight of the book brought back all his desire to try harder. Maybe it would take a whole lifetime, but it would be worth it, if only to paint one perfect picture. Magnus Macduff, artist.

'I have Andrew Murray's copy, too,' said the Duke, hunting amongst the parcels. 'Perhaps it would be better if you took it to him yourself. He would appreciate that.' He gave Magnus a keen look. 'Will you do it, boy?'

'I might,' said Magnus, taking the parcel and laying it on the table.

'Right!' said the Duke, not pressing the point. He knew that Magnus could be led but not driven. 'Now tell me about that boy upstairs.'

'Him!' cried Magnus. 'Goodness! I forgot about his supper.'

He hastily poured some milk into a small pan and set it by the fire to heat.

'What is he like?' asked the Duke curiously.

'Like?' Magnus thought for a moment. He was not sure what Lionel was like. 'He's English.'

'Oh!' said the little man, giving Magnus a knowing look. 'So you don't like him?'

'Well!' It was true that Magnus had not liked him at first. Now he was not so sure. 'Och! He's not bad,' he said gruffly, and poured out the hot milk into one of Gran's thick tumblers. 'Come on up, Duke, and see him for yourself.'

'Right! I'll carry the tray if you take the lamp.'

Magnus lighted the way while the Duke stepped over the packages in the lobby and climbed the steep creaking stairs. He was halfway up when he stopped suddenly and almost let the tray drop from his hands.

'What's up, Duke?'

'Listen!' There was a look of sheer astonishment on the Duke's face. 'Don't you recognize it, boy?'

Magnus listened. He could hear Lionel singing in a clear sweet voice. There were no words, but surely there was something familiar about the air. Something he had heard often before in the Tower room at Cronan Castle.

Suddenly he knew. 'It's out of your *Sula Symphony*,' he said to the Duke.

'That's it! Bless my soul! How did *he* know? Come along, Magnus; let's find out.'

5 Christmas in Sula

Lionel was sitting up in bed with Gran's knitted shawl over his shoulders. He was still looking peaky, but it seemed that, like the District Nurse, he had taken the turn.

He had been singing softly to himself in the darkness, but when Magnus came in carrying the lamp he stopped.

'I say, Magnus, I'm feeling much better,' he began. Then he stared in surprise at the Duke who had come in at Magnus's heels.

The Duke stared back. 'How did you know that music?' he asked, dumping the tray on the bedside table and coming straight to the point. 'Where did you hear it before?'

'In London. It's your *Sula Symphony*.'

'Mercy me!' gasped Magnus. 'Fancy you being there, at the performance. You never said.'

'You never asked,' said Lionel simply.

There was a lot more he might have said, about how he had tried to make closer contact with Magnus and how the boy from Sula had always brushed him off. Now he turned to the Duke and looked at him with shining eyes. 'It's the most wonderful music. It keeps haunting me. I never thought I would be lucky enough to meet the composer. But I was determined to see Sula after hearing your music. It was like a picture. I could see the island so clearly. The seals, the seabirds; and I could hear the wind whistling . . .'

'You must be a musician yourself to feel like that,' said the little Duke, beaming at the boy and sitting down by the bedside. He had received many tributes but none as simple and sincere as this. 'Tell me about yourself.'

Magnus had a sudden feeling of being left out. The Duke was his own special property. Now he and the London boy were talking together as if they were old friends. Lionel was telling about his great love of music, how he was having his voice trained, and that his great ambition was to be an operatic singer.

'You'll do it!' cried the little Duke. 'No reason why not, if you work hard enough.' He turned to Magnus. 'Don't you agree, boy?'

'Drink your milk,' said Magnus sulkily, and thrust the tumbler at Lionel.

The Duke saw the expression on Magnus's face and understood.

'*He*'s the chap who helped me,' he told Lionel. 'That's what we all need. Someone to have faith in us. Who have you got?'

'My mother,' said Lionel, with a warm note in his voice. 'My father's dead, but she and I are very close. She believes in me. Only there's no money. Mother goes out to work, and I'll do the same as soon as I'm old enough. Singing lessons cost a lot. But we'll see.'

The Duke rubbed his chin. 'Yes, we'll see!' He looked at Magnus. 'You and I will have to put our heads together, boy.'

Magnus still looked strained. He was not too sure that he approved of this sudden interest the Duke was taking in the London boy.

'How would you like another trip to London?' the little man asked him.

'Me?' said Magnus.

'Yes, you. Wouldn't dream of going without you. The thing is, they want to record the *Symphony*, and they would like me to be there at the time. So I thought . . .'

'Good!' cried Lionel from the bed. 'That means everyone will be able to hear it played over and over again. I say, Your Grace, that's wonderful!'

Magnus gave him a glower. What right had he to put in his oar? This was between the Duke and himself.

'Do come, Magnus,' cried Lionel. 'I say! I could show you round.'

'It's time you were sleeping,' said Magnus crossly, turning the lamp down.

'Time we were all sleeping,' said the little Duke, jumping up from the bedside chair. 'Can't wait till I try out that box-bed.'

Magnus was the only one in Gran's cottage who did not sleep soundly that night. He lay awake in the dark little press with his father's oilskins for company, thinking about the boy from London and wondering what it was about him that made people grow to like him. Jinty, and now the Duke. Magnus had never cared what people thought about him, but now he began to realize that it mattered to him. Perhaps he should make an effort, instead of always fending people off.

That night, as he tossed and turned, Magnus began to learn a lesson. He would have to give and take a little more. But it was not a prospect that pleased him.

Next day the news went round that the Ferret had come out in spots.

'Oh my! Isn't that awful?' said Jinty, making a meal of it. 'It'll likely be the measles or the scarlet fever and we'll all catch it. With the District Nurse ill, too.'

The Ferret himself refused to lie low. Not with so many exciting things about to happen. The thaw coming, the Duke's presents to deliver, the Christmas festivities to arrange. If the District Nurse could not come to him, he would go and consult her.

'You're a fine sight,' she told him, as he stood shuffling his feet by her bedside while she took his temperature and had a closer look at his spotty face. 'How are you feeling?'

'Fine,' said the Ferret defiantly.

'You'll live,' said Mrs Gillies, half-disappointed that it was nothing serious. 'It's only spots. Eat some of the Duke's oranges and you'll be all right.'

The Ferret ran thankfully home, grabbed an orange and dashed out again, sucking it. He felt ready for anything.

'Fight?' he called hopefully to Magnus who had just emerged from Gran's door.

Magnus shook his head. He was half-dazed after his sleepless night and still not sure what it was all about. The Duke had gone upstairs to sit by Lionel's bedside, and that strange feeling of jealousy had returned. He would have to work it out of his system.

'I've got things to deliver. Come on and help.'

'Right,' said the Ferret, throwing away his orange peel. It would be better than kicking his heels and doing nothing.

As they went from house to house, carrying the Duke's packages, they could feel the change in the atmosphere. The thaw was on. The seabirds had left their crannies and and were circling round calling to each other as if spreading the good news. The sun shone out as warm as summer, and soon the icicles began to drip and the snow to melt. Already the Duke's statue was beginning to dwindle.

The two boys were perspiring after running from door to door with their burdens.

'I'm warm,' gasped the Ferret, too exhausted now to fight but still looking for mischief. Jinty was hanging about at the Cowans' door like a knotless thread, half hoping Magnus might invite her in to visit Lionel. It was an idle hope, but Jinty never gave in. Miracles might happen.

Instead, she received a stinging blow on the cheek from a snowball fired at her by the Ferret.

'Spotty-face!' she yelled at him, rubbing the sore place. 'I'll murder you!'

The Ferret stuck his tongue out at her, then turned his attention to a new target. He had caught sight of the schoolmaster coming towards them, dragging his lame leg. An easy mark. Gloating with anticipation, he crouched down to scoop up a handful of softening snow.

Magnus saw what was happening and took swift action. 'Stop it!' he said, and pushed the Ferret so hard that he fell flat on his face in the melting snow.

The Ferret spluttered, spat out a mouthful of snow, and yelled, 'Teacher's pet!' in an enraged voice.

Magnus ignored the jibe and went forward to meet Andrew Murray. It was the only time in his life that he had made the first move. The schoolmaster looked surprised but pleased.

'Hullo, Magnus.'

'Hullo.' Magnus looked away, not wanting to meet the man's gaze. 'I've got something for you,' he said gruffly.

'Good!' said Andrew, falling into step beside him. 'I was coming to call on you and the Duke, to find out how Lionel is.'

'He's fine,' said Magnus shortly. He did not want to waste time talking about the London boy. All he wanted was to hand over the Duke's parcel containing the copy of the teacher's book, and be done with it.

Yet here he was half an hour later sitting at Gran's well-scrubbed table, side by side with the teacher, going over the book page by page. Andrew was admiring the drawings, pointing out how well they fitted into the text and improved the look of the book. Magnus was looking at them critically, thinking they were not bad but wishing he had done better. Now and again he cast his eyes on the words, reading to himself in his halting way the story of Sula as the teacher had written it.

'That's good,' he said out loud. 'That bit about the Fairy Ring on Little Sula.'

Andrew Murray felt a stab of pride, almost like an electric shock running through him. Strange how a few words of praise from the young island boy could please him so much. For the first time the barriers were down and they could converse without restraint. Specky the hen had hopped on to the table and was pecking at a crumb of oatcake. The frosty patterns on the window pane were melting, and a clearer light was coming into the kitchen. It seemed as if the dark past was being swept away.

'Magnus,' said the teacher suddenly. 'I have something to tell you. Can you keep a secret?'

'Ay, I can.'

'The fact is, Magnus,' Andrew Murray hesitated. It seemed that, for a change, it was *he* who was finding words difficult. 'The fact is, I'm going—'

'Going!' said Magnus, aghast.

He stared at the teacher in dismay, suddenly realizing how much the man meant to him. Magnus had fought against him at first, fending off all intimacy, but now they had reached some kind of understanding. Too late.

Suddenly a sound was heard.

'Not a word!' said the teacher hastily, as the Duke came bounding down the stairs, jumping the last step. He gave an approving smile when he saw Magnus and the schoolmaster sitting together.

'Well done, boy,' he said to Magnus, then he turned to Andrew Murray. 'I've had a great talk with Lionel. A remarkable chap. So full of intelligence, and what a musical ear! Perfect pitch, that's what he has. Perfect!'

Magnus closed the book with a bang and pushed back from the table.

'Where are you going, boy?' asked the little Duke in surprise.

'Out!' said Magnus, and not another word.

The black dog was on his back, as Gran said when Magnus was in a bad mood. Why was he feeling like this? Was it because of the teacher's secret, and the fact that the Duke was taking such an interest in the boy from London?

'People!' thought Magnus kicking at the melting snow. Animals were better. He would go off and try to find Old Whiskers.

The ice was melting rapidly round the edges of the sea, floating away like small icebergs over the water. Magnus watched them, thinking, '*There*'s a picture!' Then the black dog growled on his back and he kicked again at the slushy snow. He was fed up with pictures. Fed up with everything; especially Lionel and his perfect pitch!

Mr Skinnymalink, the Hermit, was wandering about on the shore, taking in great gulps of fresh air. He, more than anyone on the island, had felt hemmed in by the snow. Now he was like a caged animal let loose. Magnus and he passed each other without any words. Just a brief nod, but it was enough. There was the right kind of feeling between them.

The same feeling Magnus had for Old Whiskers.

'You're there!' he cried, and forgot all the petty

nigglings in his mind when he saw his old friend nosing
his way up out of the icy water. The seal swayed from side
to side, snuffling and grunting with pleasure. It was his
way of saying, 'Hullo! I'm glad to see you.'

Old Whiskers was pleased, not only to see the boy again,
but to feel the warmth of the wintry sun seeping through
his body. It was not yet warm enough for him to come out
and lie on the rocks. They were still covered with slippery
ice. But the day would come when he and the boy would
lie there happily, side by side. In the meantime it was best
to keep on the move.

Old Whiskers gave another grunt, turned a cartwheel
and vanished below the surface. It had been a brief
meeting but it was enough to satisfy them both. The load
had lightened from Magnus's back as he turned away from
the shore. Andrew Murray, limping home towards the

schoolhouse, saw him and gave him a friendly wave. He seemed in high spirits. His secret, whatever it was, appeared to have made him more cheerful.

Magnus hesitated for a moment. Then he waved back.

'Merry Christmas, Avizandum. I've got it!'

'What?' asked the small voice from Tair's pocket.

'The gun from Santa Claus. Remember? You were right.'

'I'm always right,' said Avizandum smugly.

Tair sat down on an upturned pail and shot everyone who passed by. Some reacted in the proper fashion. Magnus fell dead at his feet with a groan, and lay as still as a stone for a few moments before getting up and pursuing his own ploys. The Ferret hit back with a sloppy snowball; and Jinty clutched her heart, screaming. 'Help! I'm dead!' After taking a look at the melting snow, she decided not to collapse on the dirty ground. Gran, too, strode by, not taking any notice of how many shots were being fired at her.

Tair was not the only one on the island whom Santa had remembered. There were presents for everyone, some home-made, others brought by the Duke. Though his gifts were welcome, it was the more homely ones the people liked better, perhaps because they knew how much time and care had gone into the making of them. The hand-knitted scarves, the tea cosies, the rag dolls, the wooden toys.

Magnus's present from Mr Skinnymalink was a seal, carefully carved in wood.

'Old Whiskers!' cried Magnus in delight, and held it in his hand like a treasure. He took it home and set it on the mantelpiece beside Gran's tea-caddy. Every time he looked at it he felt a glow of pleasure.

He was not a giver of presents himself, except for two. One for Gran, one for the Duke. Both were pictures which he had painted himself. He hung Gran's up on the kitchen wall and waited to hear her reactions. When she came clattering in with a pail in her hand she caught sight of it and stared at it in surprise.

'What's that?' she said, dumping the pail on the floor.

'A present for you, Gran.'

'Mercy me!'

Gran gazed at it in silence. She was not looking at a picture but at herself. And yet, was it herself? Was that how Magnus saw her, with the hint of a smile on her face? The wrinkles were there, the plain countenance, the grey hair pulled tightly back from the forehead. But that smile! The picture began to blur and the old woman realized she was looking at it through a mist of tears.

'Thanks, laddie,' she said huskily, and turned away. But she looked back at the picture every now and again, and kept it hanging there. And throughout the day her smile was seen more often.

The Duke's was a more complicated picture. It had begun in Magnus's head the night he sat in the great London concert hall and listened to the orchestra playing the *Sula Symphony*. As he watched the conductor wielding his baton and saw how the musicians followed the beat, the whole world seemed to be filled with harmony and colour. The Duke had woven a perfect pattern in his composition, one that Magnus longed to achieve in his painting.

He had tried. He began by depicting the members of the orchestra as he had seen them; as people. But suddenly it seemed they had all turned into beasts and birds. It was Old Whiskers who held the baton. The 'cellists were puffins, the fiddlers razor-bills. There were hares, rabbits,

hedgehogs, cormorants, ducks, all playing different
instruments. Seagulls turned the pages of the score with
their wings; crabs crawled about carrying musical notes in
in their mouths; a dolphin beat the big drum. Even the
baton itself turned into a wriggling eel.

The Duke was enchanted with the picture. 'Can't wait
to hang it up in the Castle,' he cried, gloating over all the
details. 'It's a brilliant piece of work. Brilliant. I'll treasure
it all my life. Thank you, boy.'

Magnus felt a warm glow. He would sooner have a kind
word from the Duke than have the whole world thinking
him a genius. They were back on their old terms again,
and Magnus could even give a friendly greeting to Lionel
when he came downstairs, still looking pale and wan. 'But
I'm coming to the Christmas party,' he declared.

It was held, as all Sula sprees were, in the schoolroom,
with the desks shoved to the side and the blackboard
turned to the wall. There was no tree, no holly, no tinsel;
none of the usual trappings of Christmas. But the spirit
was there. It was not only a jollification to celebrate
Christmas but a thanksgiving now that the snow-siege was
ended.

The food was laid out on a trestle-table, pride of place
being given to the Christmas cake, encrusted with icing,
which the Duke had brought with him. The rest of the
food was homely enough. Oatcakes, plain scones, rock
buns, mince pies, and a great urn of tea to wash it all
down. Everyone had baked what they could from their
meagre supplies, and Gran had managed to produce a
large dumpling with 'mindings' inside. Mother-of-pearl
buttons, a silver coin, a thimble, a small ring.

Jinty, trigged out in her best blue velvet frock with
ribbons in her hair, blushed scarlet when she fell heir to
the ring. It was an omen! If it had been the thimble she

would have been doomed to be an old maid. She looked coyly at Magnus, then at Lionel. Two strings to her bow. Jinty's cup was overflowing.

Old Cowan had brought his melodeon – his squeeze box – and the Duke borrowed an old fiddle. The merry music set everyone's feet tapping, and before long they were all whirling round the schoolroom dancing Eightsome Reels, Schottisches and Highland Flings.

At the end, the minister mopped his brow and reminded them that this was Christmas. A holy time.

'So let us sing some carols.'

Lionel's clear true voice could be heard above the others', ringing out the old familiar tunes – *Hark the Herald Angels Sing, Away in a Manger, O Come All Ye Faithful*.

There was a lump in Magnus's throat as he listened. He was aware of a change inside him, but what kind of change he could not tell. He looked at Gran and saw that the faint smile was on her face. Maybe there was going to be a change in her, too.

And the schoolmaster. The look on *his* face seemed to foretell a happier future.

6 New Beginnings

Matthew, Mark, Luke, John and Rebecca were having their first outing. Under the watchful eye of Blackie, their proud mother, they had crawled out of their basket and were starting to explore the world.

It was the minister who had christened them. After all, they were Manse kittens and ought to have suitable names. The problem was what to do with them. He could put up with one cat, but not six.

'Drown them,' said the Ferret, relishing the thought. 'It's quite easy,' he told Magnus. The two boys were hanging over the garden wall that surrounded the Manse garden. There was still some patching up to be done to the house, but the minister and his wife were back in residence, and Blackie and her tribe were making little forays towards the rockery.

'You just put them in a sack with a stone in the bottom, and chuck them into the sea,' explained the Ferret.

'I'll chuck you into the sea,' threatened Magnus. He was drawing pictures in his mind's eye of the furry little creatures tumbling over each other. Then suddenly he made up his mind. 'I'll find homes for them.'

'It would be better fun drowning them,' grumbled the Ferret.

Magnus punched him on the nose, then ran off on his mission of mercy. First to Mrs McCallum's. Yes! She would take one. Tair and the twins would enjoy playing with a wee kitten.

Old Morag McLeod, too, would like one for company.

Her old tabby had died last year. And the District Nurse grudgingly agreed to take in Luke. 'But not till I feel a bit stronger myself,' she told Magnus. 'Kittens can take an awful lot out of you. Worse than bairns.'

The remaining two were more difficult to place. Jinty wanted one, chiefly to curry favour with Magnus, but old Cowan firmly said NO. Not with Rory, the collie, around. 'It would have a dog's life,' said he, mixing his metaphors.

What about Gran? Magnus found it more difficult to ask her than the others. He took Rebecca with him, the most attractive of the lot, a white bundle of fur. But he had a good idea what Gran's answer would be.

'No! I have enough beasts to look after already.'

'Oh Gran! Look! She's only a wee thing. I'll take care of her.'

'You!' She gave the boy a withering look. 'You're never here. Always gadding away with Himself.'

Magnus took a quick look at her. What did Gran mean? Could *she* be jealous, too? If so, he knew what the feeling was like.

'I'd sooner be here, Gran,' he said quietly, and turned his head to look at the picture on the wall. Gran looked at it, too. Then her face grew softer and she held out her hands for the kitten.

'Och well, laddie,' she said, and no more; but it was enough. Rebecca had found a home.

There was only Matthew left, the coal-black one. 'Tell you what, boy,' said the little Duke, 'we'll take him home with us. There's plenty of room in the Castle, and Bella can look after him when we go to London.'

London! Magnus suddenly realized that this peaceful period on the island would soon be over. He would like best to stay for ever and always in Sula with Gran and old Whiskers; but he knew there could be no turning back. He must return to Cronan with the Duke and continue his studies at the High School. He was only beginning to find out from the Art Master how much he had still to learn about drawing and painting.

There was an air of restlessness and movement on the island as if the melting snow had released everyone from a spell. Once more the fishing boats could go out. Magnus could row across to Little Sula. The sheep began to wander about on the Heathery Hill looking for tasty bites to eat. Best of all, the *Hebridean* came bumping into the pier, bringing mail and fresh supplies of food.

Magnus and the Duke would be leaving with it on its next visit, but now there was only one passenger going away. Lionel's holiday was over, and it was time for him to return to London. He was still looking pale as he carried his case up the gangway. But his eyes were bright as he hung over the side to take a last look at Sula and to wave good-bye to the group of people who had gathered on the shore.

'I'll see you in London,' he called to Magnus.

'Huh!' said Magnus; but he waved back. Now that Lionel was going, he realized he would miss him.

Jinty had turned on the waterworks. It was one of her big scenes. The deserted heroine saying farewell to her lover. 'You'll come back, won't you?' she gulped, looking tearfully up at Lionel. 'Send me a p-post-c-card.'

She was hiccupping by now as she reached the height of her performance. It was a pity the self-raising flour she had dabbed on her nose was beginning to run. But Lionel was not looking at her. He was gazing beyond, at the Heathery Hill and all the peaceful scenes he was leaving behind.

The boat gave a blast and began to back clumsily away from the pier. Jinty sighed, rubbed the tears and the flour off her face, and turned her attention to Magnus. Her first love.

'Magnus,' she began, still waving to the disappearing Lionel, 'I've got something to tell you.' She paused for effect and then fired the shot. 'When you go back to Cronan, I'm coming too.'

'What?' said Magnus, alarmed.

'Yes! I thought you would be pleased. I spoke to Mr Murray about going to the Girls' High School and he says I can. I'm bright enough. Isn't it great?'

She was bright, all right! Magnus could almost hear her brain ticking like a busy little clock. She chattered on and on, though he was hardly listening, about her new school-uniform, what her classmates would be like, and how she was planning to see all the sights of Cronan. Finally about where she was going to live. Her dearest wish was to become Miss Jinty Cowan of Cronan Castle. But she knew it would be no use approaching the Duke himself.

'Couldn't you speak to His Grace, Magnus?' she asked in a wheedling voice.

'No,' said Magnus, flatly and firmly.

The very thought of Little Miss Know-All poking into every corner made him squirm. It would be the end of their peace, of the quiet times he and the Duke shared in the Tower.

'No!' he repeated in a louder voice, in case she had not heard.

'Oh well,' said Jinty. She was used to being rejected, and perhaps she could work on Magnus later, once she was living in Cronan. 'There's always the Reekies. I can stay at Rockview with them. And the great thing is, I can see you every day, Magnus.'

Magnus wished the boat would reverse and bring Lionel back, but it had already rounded Sula Point and there was nothing left of it but the wake in the water.

He had only one more week left in which to savour the quiet joys of Sula. It was one of the happiest he had ever spent. The air was clear and cold. He could almost taste it, like the buttermilk he drank after Gran had been doing the churning. Soor dook, she called it.

Everything he saw delighted his artist's eye. The pale wintry colourings, the wide expanse of sky, the starkness of the rocks, the grey-blue of the sea, the dark brown of the withered bracken.

Magnus wandered on the shore, picking up cowrie shells that looked like painted teeth with white gums, and finding small crabs in the pools. He watched the guillemots, a study in black and white, clustering together on the rocks, the ducks dibbling in the water, the gulls pecking and feeding on the surface, and Old Nick diving after his prey. This was the sailors' name for the greedy cormorant who filched the fish before their very eyes.

He watched people, too, absorbed in their tasks. Old Cowan mending the dyke, Gran baking a scone, the Hermit carving a figure out of a chunk of wood. They were all artists in their own way, striving to do something well, as he himself tried when he was painting a picture. Surely it would be better to stay here, amongst quiet folk, than to go out into the stirring world. But he knew this could only be an interval, all the more precious because it would pass so soon.

At night he sat at the table in the lamplit kitchen poring over the teacher's book, while Gran sat by the fire with her mending. They spoke little, but now and then they looked at each other. Back in his own bed, Magnus was lulled to sleep by the surge of the sea rolling in to the shore, and floated off to sleep with a great sense of well-being.

On the last day he went to the school. No badgering from the teacher. No cajoling from Jinty. He just went.

It was Jinty's last day, too, and she was out to make the most of it. She had turned up in full regalia to show off her new uniform to the rest of the class. Navy-blue skirt and jumper, school hat, blazer complete with badge. Cronan High School for Girls. A perfect picture.

She had bought a large bag of sweets from the Cowans' shop to hand round to everyone. Liquorice allsorts, caramels, jujubes, dolly-mixtures, peppermint creams. Like Lady Bountiful, she spread them around, placing a whipped cream walnut on the teachers' desk as a special offering. Andrew Murray took no notice of it.

'Sit down, Jinty Cowan,' he said sternly.

He was marking the register, and as far as he was concerned this was going to be an ordinary day. Except that he had a letter in his breast-pocket – next to his heart – that gave a lift to his feelings every time he thought of it. And how could it be an ordinary day when he looked up and saw Magnus sitting in his old place? Andrew found it difficult to conceal his pleasure. He had scored a victory, but he tried not to gloat.

At first the lesson went on normally, as normally as possible with such a mixed range of pupils to teach.

Tair, prompted by Avizandum, got up to say his poetry:

'Faster than fairies, faster than witches,
Bridges and houses, hedges and britches . . .'
'Ditches!' corrected Avizandum.

The Ferret was glowering at the sums on the blackboard and mentally rubbing them out with a duster. Black Sandy was pencilling in a moustache on Mary Queen of Scots in his history book, while Red Sandy was pretending to study geography even though his book was upside down. Jinty was sucking a lemon drop and clearing out a lifetime of sweetie papers from her desk. Magnus was doing nothing, except looking and feeling, taking in everything around him to retain in his mind and carry away with him.

He caught the teacher's eye and did not look away. It was only for a fleeting moment, but there was something in the boy's direct gaze that made Andrew Murray feel happy. At long last he was breaking through the boy's resistance.

Andrew felt a surge of pleasure, as if new life was pulsing through his veins. His lame leg felt less painful when he stood up. He sensed that this was a time to do something special, to forget ordinary lessons and make this a day to remember.

'What about a story?'

'Oh, yessir, please, sir!'

Andrew had the true art of story-telling. Even the

Ferret would sit still, hanging on his every word. Especially if the story was about the big beasts. The great dinosaurs striding up the Heathery Hill, the brontosaurus 'sixty feet long and weighing twenty tons', the giant lizards walking on their hind legs, using their dagger-like thumbs as weapons.

But today the story was not about the big beasts. It was a simple story about a boy. Magnus sat doodling idly on the margin of his jotter, then laid down his pencil and listened intently. Who was the teacher talking about? A boy who had been brought up in a big city, pampered and petted by rich parents, given an expensive education, a boy who was expected to make his mark in the world.

'Please sir, what was the boy's name, sir?' Jinty Cowan, as usual wanting to know everything.

'He was just a boy,' said Andrew, gazing out of the window as if seeing the boy in the story instead of a peaceful view of the harbour. 'A boy who grew up to be a young man full of ambition to conquer the world, to become a famous explorer, perhaps, or an inventor; even a Prime Minister. Then suddenly one day something happened.'

He stopped and drew in his breath.

'What?' asked Magnus, not knowing he had spoken out loud.

Andrew Murray fixed his gaze on him but he was thinking of that other boy. 'He was stricken with an illness and all his dreams vanished . . .'

'Oooooooh!' said the class in a sympathetic murmur.

'Instead of making his way in the world he was forced to go to a remote place in search of health.' The teacher's voice brightened. 'And there he found something far better than fame or fortune. Peace and happiness . . .'

Yes! thought Magnus. The man was speaking about

himself. But if he had found peace and happiness here in Sula why was he going away? Suddenly he stopped listening, grabbed his pencil and angrily drew a black dog in his jotter. The black dog that Gran said was sometimes on his back.

After a while he was aware that the story had come to an end. Andrew's last words were 'happily ever after,' as if he was finishing a fairy-tale. 'I'd sooner have heard about the big beasts,' muttered the Ferret, feeling cheated.

When it was time to leave, Jinty turned on the tears. Real tears this time. It had suddenly struck her that this was the end of a chapter. Never again would she sit in her familiar place in the schoolroom side by side with the friends of her childhood. Never again would she kick the Ferret under the desk when he was aiming inky pellets at her. Never again would she be the first to thrust up her hand and say eagerly, 'Please, sir, I know the answer, sir.'

She was sure of her ground here, queen of all she surveyed. But what of the future, in a strange classroom, with no sight of the harbour from the window and no friendly faces to be seen? Even her shabby old desk held a sentimental value now that she was leaving it for ever. The sight of her initials gouged out with Black Sandy's pocket knife was too much for her. The bag of sweets and her new blazer could not console her. Jinty put down her head and howled.

'Now then, Jinty,' said Andrew Murray, coming towards her. But he understood and patted her gently on the head. 'Don't worry, it's going to be all right. You'll enjoy the new school at Cronan, and I know you will be a credit to us all. After all, it's a real feather in your cap.'

'Yes, so it is,' said Jinty, raising her tearful face from the desk and quickly regaining her composure. 'Would you like a jujube, Mr Murray?'

'Yes, thank you,' said Andrew, accepting it from her crumpled paper bag. 'Good-bye, Jinty, and good luck.' He shook hands with her and then called out to Magnus, who was making for the door. 'Magnus, wait. I have something to tell you.'

7 Life in London

Magnus shuffled his feet uneasily, ready to dart out of the door the moment the teacher was finished with him. Why had Andrew Murray asked him to stay behind?

'You remember I was going to tell you a secret, Magnus?' said Andrew, taking an envelope from his breast pocket.

'Uh-huh!' said Magnus, giving him one of his old hostile looks. If the man had decided to go away, let him go. Who cared?

Deep down in his heart Magnus realized that *he* cared. He had become used to this gentle schoolmaster who had taken such an interest in his painting, and had grown to like him. But he was not going to show it.

Andrew was taking a photograph out of the envelope.

'Do you remember her, Magnus?'

Magnus stared at the picture. A lovely young woman with fair hair smiled back at him. Yes! he remembered her. She had come to Sula that time the film-crew were taking pictures on the island. Diana Somebody.

'Diana Maxwell,' said Andrew with a warm note in his voice. 'Did you like her, Magnus?'

'Uh-huh!' But it was more than his usual 'Uh-huh!' Diana Maxwell had been the first person to get under his skin, to understand why he resented people pushing him around, why he liked to be alone, and that he could be led but not driven. 'Oh yes! I liked her.'

'I like her too, Magnus,' said Andrew softly. 'In fact, she's coming to live in Sula. With me.'

Magnus gave him a quick look. 'But I thought you were going away?'

'Going away? Oh no! Not when I have found such a peaceful haven as this, and such a wonderful person to share it with me. Diana and I are going to be married. That's my secret. She loves the island, and I—well, I love her. So that's it. I thought you would like to know, Magnus.'

It took the boy a few moments to collect his thoughts. Then: 'That's great!' he said. 'Great!' he repeated and shook the teachers' hand as if the two were sealing a bargain.

Yes, it was great, thought Magnus, as he flew through the air in a jet, high above the clouds. It would be wonderful having Diana on the island, a young woman with a free spirit like his own. Wonderful, too, not to lose the schoolmaster just when they had reached an understanding. Life in Sula would be even better in future.

Yet here he was, flying away from home. But only for the time being.

The clouds below him looked as if they were made of cotton wool, fluffy white tinged with pink. It would be wonderful to get out and walk amongst them on his bare feet, Magnus thought. But he was hemmed in by his safety-belt.

'There may be a little turbulence later on, so we advise you to keep your seat-belts fastened.' A voice – the Captain's – had made the announcement over the intercom.

The turbulence, when it came, was only a little bobbing up and down. The Duke, sitting beside Magnus, did not appear to notice it. He was absorbed in his music score, humming little snatches to himself and taking no notice of the rest of the passengers. Magnus, too, did not mind the uneasy motion. He had taken many a worse buffeting crossing from the mainland on the *Hebridean*.

Magnus had a sudden sinking feeling of homesickness as he stared out of the window at the clouds. That one was shaped like Little Sula, and there was Old Whiskers rearing up out of the sea, with the Heathery Hill in the background. If he half-closed his eyes he could see prehistoric monsters like the ones the teacher had spoken about.

The sinking feeling remained long after the turbulence passed. Magnus closed his eyes and saw Gran at the pier waving him good-bye. She had never waved before, only looked. But this time there had been more warmth in her parting, more reluctance to see him go.

'Watch yourself, laddie,' she said, with a break in her voice as he turned to walk up the gangway.

Magnus had a sudden urge to throw his arms round her neck, but that would have been too much. 'Watch yourself, too, Gran,' he said huskily.

They exchanged glances, and that was that. But he had noticed as the boat backed away from the pier that Gran looked frailer, that her shoulders were more bent, and that there was a hint of tears glistening in her eyes.

The air hostess was bringing round little plastic trays. It seemed strange to be eating a meal away up here above the clouds. Cold ham, lettuce, and bits of gherkin. Magnus had no appetite for them; he would sooner have had a plate of Gran's stovies.

'Tasteless rubbish,' said the Duke, pushing his tray aside. At which point a steward appeared at his side.

'The Captain's compliments, Your Grace, and would you care to come forward?'

'Forward? Oh you mean, the cockpit.' The Duke turned to Magnus. 'What about you, boy? Would you like to come?'

'Uh-huh!' said Magnus. 'I would.'

The excitement of it chased away the last feeling of homesickness. When he followed the Duke forward he caught his breath at the beauty of the scene. A whole new world lay before him, stretching into eternity.

He was not interested in the gadgets the Captain was showing him. All he wanted was to look into the distance and watch the changing pattern of the clouds below: castles, camels, pyramids, polar bears, towering mountain peaks. Then, as the plane began its descent, there was a sudden sight of land below, of a ribbon of river, and a procession of toy cars moving along a roadway.

Back in their seats, ready for landing, the little Duke turned to him and said, 'Well, this is it, boy. London!' He screwed up his nose. 'I would sooner be landing in Sula. But, never mind, we'll make the best of it.'

That night Magnus looked out from the hotel window high above Hyde Park, at the ceaseless traffic coming and going. The flickering lights looked like Willy Wisps. Did no one ever stay at home, he wondered, and wished himself back in that quiet limbo above the clouds.

There was little peace here. The constant shrilling of the telephone was driving the Duke demented in the adjoining room. He came through to Magnus, his hair ruffled and a hysterical note in his voice when he spoke.

'Can't stand it another minute! Come and take over, Magnus. Say No to everybody. NO!'

Magnus had no liking for the telephone himself, but he sat on the bed and said No to all the incoming requests for interviews and information about the Duke. Then he heard a voice that was familiar.

'Is that you, Magnus? It's Lionel.'

'Hullo,' said Magnus cautiously.

The old feeling of jealousy began to niggle at him and he looked furtively at the Duke. The little man was busy unpacking his case, bringing out his favourite fiddle so that he could seek solace in music. It seemed strange to hear the strains of the *Sula Symphony* here in this alien hotel room with its pink bedspreads, built-in wardrobes, and central heating.

'I can hear music,' Lionel was saying over the telephone. 'Is that the Duke?'

'Uh-huh!' said Magnus. 'But he's not speaking to anybody.' He added under his breath, 'not even to you.'

'That's all right,' said Lionel mildly. 'It's you I wanted to speak to, Magnus. I was wondering if you would like me to take you round London tomorrow to see the sights.'

Magnus hesitated. He wanted to see the sights, all right, but in his own way. Yet it would be helpful to have someone to show him the ropes. Someone who had been to Sula, who knew all the people there, and who had even slept in his own bed in Gran's cottage.

As if sensing what was going on, the little Duke waved his bow in the air and said, 'I'll be stuck in that rehearsal hall all day tomorrow. So if you want to go out and explore ...'

'Okay!' said Magnus into the telephone.

'Right! I'll call for you at the hotel in the morning,' Lionel told him.

On his previous visit to London there had been no time for sightseeing. But now Magnus was making up for it.

If only Gran could see him now, she would never believe her eyes! How could anyone who had never been farther away than Cronan imagine such a scene?

Magnus was riding down into the bowels of the earth on a staircase that never stopped moving. It was frightening yet thrilling. On the other side, people were passing him on their way up. It was like an endless belt.

As he watched the people moving past him and looked at the advertisements on each side, it seemed to Magnus that he was living in a confused dream. He had a sudden feeling of panic when he reached the bottom and found himself on a crowded platform. What if he lost Lionel?

'This way!' he heard a voice calling to him. 'Come along, Magnus, this is our train.'

There was no room to sit down in the crowded carriage. The train went swaying on its underground way like a mole burrowing through the earth. People were standing jammed together, trying to read their newspapers as they sped from one station to another. How could they remain strangers, in such close contact?

Magnus was thankful when Lionel pushed his way off and they went surging upwards on another moving staircase. He took a gulp of air and blinked his eyes like a pit-pony when they emerged into the sunshine.

'Trafalgar Square,' said Lionel, leading him towards the fountain.

Magnus looked up at Nelson on his Monument, then at the plump pigeons pecking on the ground. Only a statue could remain oblivious to the restless movement of the traffic and the confused sounds of the people milling to and fro.

'Keep still!' Magnus wanted to shout. 'Quiet!'

He sat by the fountain trying to still his own thoughts. Lionel at least was no chatterbox. He had enough sense to leave Magnus alone and give him time to take in the scene. And suddenly, as if a veil was lifted from his eyes, the boy from Sula saw there was beauty in it. Not the wild beauty of his own island but something more vivid, like a splash of bright colour from his paint box.

There was music, too, in the air. Not the call of the curlew or the surge of the sea, but a cacophony of sounds which a composer might well capture in a *City Symphony*. Beauty in sights and sounds was not something that belonged only to Sula.

The people, too, were human beings, different from Gran and old Cowan, but each with his own hopes and thoughts and purposes. Who was he to pass judgment on them? Magnus had a sudden desire to make contact with them, to shout out 'Hullo' to each passer-by, but it was an impulse quickly stifled.

The moment of revelation soon passed but it was not forgotten. In future Magnus was more wary of coming to quick conclusions about people and places. *His* way of living was not the only one.

For ever after he was to remember that scene in Trafalgar Square, with the fat pigeons, the passing people playing their transistors, the taxis screeching round corners, and Nelson standing solidly on his plinth. In after years it was to be the subject of one of Magnus Macduff's finest paintings.

'What next?' asked Lionel.

'The river,' said Magnus, without hesitation.

Lionel led him down to the Embankment so that he could look his fill at the Thames, with tug-boats and steamers chugging to and fro under the bridges. Magnus gazed at the Houses of Parliament where the laws of the land were made, and listened to Big Ben striking the hour.

It was the river that fascinated him most, so different from the small streams on Sula or the great Atlantic rolling in to the quiet beach. Yet, here, too, was beauty of a different kind. There were no seals to be seen nor

puffins perching on the rocks; but there was one brave
seagull sitting on the water. Magnus felt akin to it, as if
they were both out of their depth.

'Museums or art galleries?' Lionel suggested next. But
Magnus shook his head. He wanted to see them on his
own, or maybe with the Duke.

'All right, then,' said Lionel amiably, 'let's go to
Buckingham Palace.'

Magnus stood at the gates and stared in at the great
building, bigger by far than Cronan Castle and in better
condition, with no crumbling walls or weedy driveway.
The flag was flying to show that royalty was in residence,
but it did not look as if real people could live there. Was
there a tower room, Magnus wondered, to which

monarchs could escape when they wanted to forget the cares of state?

Lionel guided him all over London, in and out of tubes and buses, till he had seen the Tower, the City, Piccadilly Circus and the Albert Hall, as well as street markets and a colourful quarter called Soho. His head was whirling. It had been a long day and it would take ages to sort out the kaleidoscope of strange scenes.

In the bus on the way back to the hotel it struck Magnus that Lionel had said little about himself.

'Are you getting on all right?' he asked.

'Getting on?'

'With your music.'

'Oh, that!' Lionel tried to keep a light note in his voice as he said, 'I had to give up the lessons. No money. Never mind, I still practise, and, of course, I listen to music whenever I get the chance.'

Magnus said nothing, but he made up his mind to tell the Duke that night while they were having their meal together in the great dining-room of the hotel.

It was like the inside of a palace, with glittering chandeliers hanging overhead and soft music playing in the distance. Waiters kept coming and going, bringing menus listing strange foods such as Magnus had never heard of before. Scampi, escargots, crêpes suzettes. He would sooner have had one of Gran's oatcakes and a refreshing drink of soor dook.

The little Duke's tie was askew and he had a faraway look on his face as if he was still hearing music inside his head.

'Is it going all right, Duke?' Magnus asked him.

'Going?' said the Duke, coming back to earth. 'Oh yes, I think so, boy. You must come with me tomorrow when they're doing the recording.' He smoothed down his hair and beamed across the table at Magnus. 'How did you get on today?'

'All right,' said Magnus. He might tell the Duke later about what he had seen in the great stirring city, but not now. He wanted to talk about Lionel instead.

'He's not getting on with his music. He can't afford lessons,' Magnus blurted out.

'Who?' The Duke waved away a waiter and concentrated on what Magnus was telling him. 'You mean that boy, Lionel? He mustn't give it up. We'll have to see about it.'

'Yes,' said Magnus, sitting back with a satisfied look on his face. In some way he felt that he had vindicated himself. By bringing Lionel's plight to the Duke's notice he had rid himself of the jealousy he had felt on the island. He knew the Duke would keep his word. Something would be done.

Next morning there was a letter for him. From Jinty Cowan. It was headed Rockview, Cronan, where she was staying with her relatives, the Reekies.

Jinty was as voluble on paper as she was in real life. She had hardly had time to settle down at the High School, yet she knew everything already. All the same, Magnus sensed a feeling of homesickness between the lines, a feeling he knew only too well himself.

'I went down to the harbour to have a keek at the *Hebridean*,' she wrote. 'Captain Campbell was getting ready to sail, so I gave him a lot of messages for everybody. The Reekies are very kind, but Auntie Jessie's leg is still bad. They were asking for you, Magnus, and wondering when you were coming back. Me, too. It'll be great seeing you. The school is all right. I can do the lessons fine. My new teacher, Mrs Gillespie, says I'm very quick. Some of the other girls are a bit slow . . .'

Magnus skipped a few lines, but when he saw Gran's name he sat up and took notice.

'Captain Campbell was saying that Gran was coming across to Cronan.'

Gran going to Cronan! What on earth for?

'She has to see the doctor at the Cottage Hospital. But it's nothing much, so you're not to worry.'

Not to worry?

Magnus pushed his breakfast aside and went as white as the hotel tablecloth. He was thinking of his last sight of Gran, looking frailer than usual as she waved him good-bye.

'Anything the matter, boy?' asked the Duke, looking up from his poached egg.

'It's Gran. She's not well. She's at the Cottage Hospital.' Magnus looked across at the Duke in despair.

'Bless my soul!' The Duke ruffled his hair. 'We must do something about it. Let me think.' He drummed his fingers on the table for a moment and then made up his mind. 'Tell you what, boy. I'll put through a call to the hospital and find out what's what.'

'Oh, that's great, Duke,' said Magnus, with a note of relief in his voice. 'Thanks.'

They went up in the lift to the Duke's bedroom. Magnus sat on the bed, biting his fingers, while the little man put through the call. The Duke's conversations were always short and sharp.

'Dr McGregor? Good! Can you give me any news of Mrs Macduff? *Macduff*. From Sula.'

Magnus held his breath as he listened to the Duke's side of the conversation.

'H'm! Is she? How long? When? Yes, I see. Well, thank you, Doctor. Goodbye!'

When he laid down the receiver Magnus looked at him imploringly, hardly daring to ask, 'Is she— is she very ill?'

'No, nothing to worry about,' the Duke reassured him. 'She just took a little turn.'

'A turn?'

'Her heart. Overworked. All she needs is a rest. She was taken across to the Cottage Hospital for an examination. Dr McGregor says she'll be all right if she lies still for a while.'

Gran lying still! Magnus could not picture her in the Hospital. Gran who had never had a single day's illness in her hard-working life.

'I'll have to go,' he said, jumping up. 'I must see Gran.'

8 Magnus Makes up his Mind

He was hurrying along the road from Cronan Castle on his way to visit Gran in the Cottage Hospital.

In his hand he carried a great bunch of flowers which the Duke's gardener had picked for him. Bronze and golden chrysanthemums grown in one of the broken-down old greenhouses.

Magnus had another present for Gran in his pocket which he had bought before he left London. It was a brooch, plain because he knew Gran did not like anything fancy, in the shape of a lover's knot. It was just something personal to give her. A small minding.

His heart was thumping as he neared the gates and saw the hospital ahead. He had been in there himself as a patient, but that was nothing. He could cope with his own suffering. It was worse – much worse – seeing someone else suffer without being able to help them. Someone he loved.

'Yoo-hoo, Magnus!'

Magnus whipped round and saw a schoolgirl running eagerly towards him. Jinty Cowan. The last person he wanted to see at that moment, but there was no escape.

Jinty was swinging her school satchel as she ran towards him. 'Wait, Magnus, wait!' When she reached his side she clutched at his arm and breathed, 'Oh my! It's great to see you again, Magnus.' For one dreadful moment he feared she was about to kiss him.

Real tears welled up into her eyes. It was not so much seeing him as seeing someone from Sula that had roused her emotion. Even Jinty, usually so sure of herself, felt the tug of home.

'Are you away to see Gran?'

'Uh-huh!'

'Would you like me to come with you?' she asked hopefully.

Magnus shook his head. 'No!' He wanted to see Gran on his own.

'Do you think she's going to die?' asked Jinty with her customary lack of tact.

'No, she's not!' said Magnus in a cross voice. But the very thought of it made his blood run cold. 'I'll have to go,' he said, and turned away.

'Will you come and visit me at the Reekies?' pleaded Jinty. 'Please!'

'Maybe.'

Jinty stood and watched him all the way up the drive. Would he turn and wave? No! Magnus plodded steadily on, thinking only of Gran. There would be plenty of time for Jinty, who was young and healthy. Gran was old and ill.

A doctor in a white coat spoke to him when he went in through the swing doors. 'Hullo, can I help you? Are you looking for someone?'

'It's Gran.'

'Gran? What name?'

'Macduff.'

'Oh, old Mrs Macduff,' said the doctor, pointing ahead. 'Along that passage. The room at the end.'

Gran was asleep. At least, her eyes were shut. Magnus had never seen her so still before, lying tucked and tidy in the hospital bed, so different from the box-bed in the kitchen at home. Gran, too, looked different, with her face in repose. The grey hair was still drawn tightly back from

her forehead and all the wrinkles were there, but she seemed more remote, as if she did not quite belong to the everyday world.

There was a small chair by the bed. Magnus sat down, still clutching the chrysanthemums, and looked at Gran's hands, for once lying idle on the white counterpane. Blue-veined and roughened, hands that had worked so hard and helped so many. A lump came to his throat and he put out his own hand to lay it gently on one of hers.

The old woman stirred and without opening her eyes said, 'You're there, laddie.'

'Yes, I'm here, Gran.'

He held her hand closer, then leant over and asked, 'How are you, Gran?'

'I'm fine, laddie.' She opened her eyes and looked at him. Then she gave a faint flicker of a smile. 'I thought you were away in London.'

'I'm back,' said Magnus. He held up the flowers. 'See! They're for you.'

'They're nice,' said Gran, turning her head to look at them.

Magnus laid them on the table and brought out a package from his pocket. 'It's a wee minding,' he told Gran, opening it out and showing her the brooch. 'From London.'

Gran said nothing, but she held the brooch in her hand. Then she closed her eyes. 'You're a good laddie. A good laddie.'

A nurse came in, as bright and clean as a new pin. Magnus looked at her, asking unspoken questions. She put her fingers to her lips and beckoned him outside.

'You're Magnus?' she said, when they were out in the corridor.

'Uh-huh! How—how is she?'

'She'll be all right,' said the nurse cheerfully, 'as long as she doesn't overstrain herself again. What does she do?'

'Do?' said Magnus.

It would be difficult to recount everything Gran did. Worked on the croft, rowed the boat, fed the beasts, milked the cow, dug up the peat, baked, cooked, and was at everyone's beck and call.

'She does plenty,' he told the nurse.

'Has she anyone to help her? Anyone who could take the load off her shoulders?'

It took Magnus only a second to make up his mind. 'Yes,' he said firmly, 'there's me.'

What did it matter about education or painting or anything else? Nothing was more important than Gran. He would stay at home and take some of the burden from her. It would be no sacrifice, for that was what his ambition had always been. To stay in Sula and be with Gran.

'That's all right then,' said the nurse, looking relieved. 'As long as she has someone to keep an eye on her she'll be fine.'

'When can she get home?' asked Magnus.

'In a week or so, but you must watch her and see that she takes things easily for a while.'

'Yes, I will,' promised Magnus. He squared his shoulders as if he were already carrying the burden. He seemed suddenly to have grown into a man.

He tiptoed back into Gran's room and sat quietly by her bedside, thinking of all the things he could do to help her. He would fetch and carry, feed the hens, milk the cow, row the sheep across to Little Sula, and just be there when Gran needed a strong hand to help her. He would even learn to bake and churn, if that would take the strain off her.

As he sat there he looked back, too, to the last hectic days he and the Duke had spent together in London. Once more he had experienced the joy of listening to the *Sula Symphony*, played by a great orchestra and recorded for all the world to hear. He felt a burst of pride for the little Duke.

'It's great!' Magnus told him. 'And it'll never be lost now. What next?'

'Next?' The Duke rubbed his hands together. 'As a matter of fact, I have a theme in my head, but it'll have to wait till I get home. Too much noise here. Too much confusion.'

Magnus had guessed from the Duke's abstracted looks that there was more music swirling through the little man's head. He knew the feeling of frustration. His own fingers were itching to seize a pencil or a paintbrush so that he could depict some of the scenes of London while they were still fresh in his mind.

But the most important thing to think about was Gran and how quickly he could get back to see her. There would be no time to visit the galleries. But they made time to visit the small flat in Hampstead where Lionel lived with his mother.

She was small and gentle, and there was an air of cheerfulness about the home in spite of its bare furnishings. There was no complaining, no self-pity, no envy of others who were better off.

'We're lucky to have each other,' Lionel's mother said, with a fond glance at her son. 'He looks so much better since his visit to Sula. Thank you both for what you did for him. He has been singing your praises ever since he came home.'

Magnus felt ashamed. What had he done for Lionel? Little enough, except to show his jealousy. Suddenly he felt a great desire to do something to help him. But it was the Duke, of course, who knew what to do. Behind His Grace's air of being absent-minded lay a cold streak of common sense.

'D'you know what I fancy right now?' said the little man. 'A cup of tea. One never gets a decent brew in a hotel. May I come and help you to make it?' he asked Lionel's mother.

Magnus guessed what the outcome of their private talk would be. If anyone could work magic, it was the little Duke. When Lionel's mother came back with the tea-tray there was a flush of pleasure on her cheeks. She said nothing; only gave her son a secret look. The Duke, too, made no comment. He was humming to himself as he brought in the teapot.

'The real stuff!' he said, smacking his lips. 'Made with *boiling* water.'

While they drank the tea, he and Lionel talked about music. The boy's eyes lit up as he listened to the Duke's account of the recording of his Symphony. 'I'll make sure you get one of the records,' the Duke promised him. 'And some day, you'll give me one of yours.'

He exchanged glances with the boy's mother, and Magnus knew that it was all settled, that private lessons had been arranged and that the Duke would foot the bill. Somehow he did not mind being left out of the conversation. Instead, he felt a glow of satisfaction for Lionel's sake.

'Good for you, Duke,' he said to the little man on the way back to their hotel.

The Duke winked at him. He was not one to make much of his good deeds. 'He's got a future before him, that boy. And so have you, Magnus.'

But what did the future matter if Gran was ill?

As Magnus sat by her bedside his reverie was broken by a noise outside the hospital, the sound of the Duke's rickety old car rumbling to a standstill on the gravel.

Magnus went to the window and waved to the little man. His Grace was dressed up in motoring gear. Goggles, helmet, leather coat, large fur gloves. He waved back to Magnus and mouthed the words. 'I'll wait till you're ready, boy.'

When Magnus turned away from the window he saw that Gran's eyes were open. Had she been awake all the time?

'You'd better go, laddie,' she said weakly.

He hesitated. 'Are you sure you'll be all right, Gran?'

The grey head nodded. 'Fine.'

'I'll come back soon, Gran.'

'Yes,' she said, and watched him as he went towards the door. He could hardly bear to leave her lying lonely there. He longed to turn back and say something to let her know how he felt. But she had closed her eyes and turned her head away.

There were many unspoken things between him and the Duke as they drove back to Cronan Castle. When the car backfired and came to a stop outside the front door, His Grace pushed back his goggles. 'Don't worry, boy,' he said, turning to Magnus. 'Things will sort themselves out.'

But they were sorted out already in Magnus's mind. Whatever happened he was going back to Sula. He would wait till the boat sailed, and go home to take care of the croft. Then when Gran was well enough, he would come back and fetch her.

He went up into the Tower room where he kept his easel and all his painting materials. He had grown attached to this quiet haven with its view of the untidy grounds and a glimpse of the sea beyond. He would have to give it up, but he felt no regret. Gran was more important.

He went to the hospital every day, morning and afternoon. With each visit he saw an improvement in Gran, till gradually she was sitting up in bed, then in an armchair, and finally he found her on her feet, walking slowly round the room with a watchful nurse by her side.

'You look great, Gran!' he cried in a delighted voice.

'Huh!' said Gran crossly. 'There's nothing the matter with me.'

That was another good sign. Gran's old sharpness was coming back.

'She'll be running the hospital in another week,' the nurse told Magnus, with a smile.

'It's high time I was home,' said Gran impatiently. 'When can I leave?'

'We'll see,' said the nurse. 'Have patience.'

It was not easy for Gran to sit with idle hands now that she was feeling so much better. On the day before the *Hebridean* sailed, Magnus went to pay her a last visit and found her worrying about the unfinished tasks she had left behind.

'I'll see to everything,' he assured her.

'But what about your schooling and your painting?'

'I can paint in Sula,' he said stoutly.

He could see that Gran was pleased, though she said no more on the subject. 'I hope that kitten's all right. The Cowans said they would look after her. She's a nice wee thing, Rebecca.'

Magnus hid a smile. It was strange how Gran had become so attached to the Manse kitten, just as old Bella at the Castle was besotted by Matthew. 'I'll take care of Rebecca, Gran, if you'll take care of yourself,' he said, rising to go but reluctant to leave her. 'The Duke's going to bring you back with the next boat. It's all arranged.'

'I could come now.'

'No, you could not. You'll have to do what the doctors and nurses say. Good-bye, Gran.'

With a sudden gesture, he flung his arms round her neck and kissed her wrinkled cheek. Then he blundered out of the door without looking back. If he had looked, he might have seen Gran sitting there with a strange expression on her face, holding her cheeks as if hanging on to the kiss.

On the last night he remembered his promise to Jinty

91

Cowan and went to call on her at Rockview. Mrs Reekie came to the door wearing a flowery overall and looking like an overblown peony-rose.

'Magnus!' she cried in a delighted voice, pulling him in over the doorstep. 'Jinty, here's your young man.'

Magnus kicked his heels on the linoleum in the hall when Jinty came scuttling towards him. He backed away out of her reach in case she was going to throw herself into his arms.

'Oh my! I'm awful glad to see you, Magnus. Come away in.'

Jinty took hold of his arm and tugged him into the crowded room where all the Reekies were gathered.

They were all speaking at the one time, except Willy Reekie, who lay back in his chair with the *Cronan Chronicle* over his face. Aunt Jessie sat with her bad leg up on a footstool, and wee Ailsa was playing a toy piano with more zest than expertise. *Three Blind Mice* over and over again, with one note missing.

The fire was too hot, the voices too loud, the room too crowded with knicknacks. But the Reekies were well-meaning and friendly. Over-friendly and cloying. Living with them was like eating chocolate-cream for breakfast and being wrapped in cotton wool all day. Magnus had not been in the room two minutes before he was fingering his collar and longing to throw open the window and let in some fresh air.

Mrs Reekie settled herself in an easy chair, smiled at Magnus and said, 'Now then, Magnus, tell us all about everything.'

Magnus could think of nothing to tell. Not that it mattered for Mrs Reekie gave him no time to answer. 'How's your Gran? When will she be getting home? And what about His Grace? My! He has fairly become

famous with that music of his. I was just saying to Willy
Reekie, wasn't I, Willy . . . ?'

It was the right place, Magnus could see, for Jinty, who
was used to noise and stir and chatter. The Reekies liked
her, too, because she always had plenty to say for herself.
She had been to the cinema that day and was full of chat
about the film she had seen. Every single detail was
recounted, not once but over and over again. Even if she
had only been as far as the garden gate, Jinty could have
made up a long story about it. Like the Reekies, she
seemed fascinated by the sound of her own voice.

Yet when Magnus rose to go, he saw a forlorn look on
her face, and sensed that the homesickness was still there.

'Oh, Magnus, have you got to go already?' she sighed,
jumping up and following him into the narrow hallway.

'Uh-huh!' said Magnus. 'I'm away.'

Jinty's lower lip began to tremble. 'When will I see you
again, Magnus?'

'Don't know.'

'I'll be back for the holidays,' she said, cheering up.
'You'll be there, in Sula?'

Magnus nodded.

'I'll send you a wee line,' said Jinty. 'Tell everybody
in Sula that I'm missing them.'

'Ay, I will,' said Magnus, and gave her a warmer look
than usual.

9 Home Without Gran

It was strange to see Sula looming up out of the sea and to know that Gran was not there, waiting for him.

Everything else was the same. The peat fire was still burning in Gran's cottage. It had not been out for over a hundred years. Old Cowan and Mr Skinnymalink had taken turns to keep it going while she was away. Specky the hen and Rebecca, the Manse kitten, were sitting together on the rug, content in each other's company. It was comforting for Magnus to find something alive in the house when he came home.

He wasted no time: before the *Hebridean* was away, he was out of his good clothes and into his old breeks and jersey, ready to start work. It seemed as if the harder he worked the sooner Gran would get well. He tried to do everything the way she liked it done, as if she were standing over him, shouting, 'Mag-nus! Mind how you empty that pail. Mag-nus! See that the kettle doesn't boil over. Mag-nus!'

By the end of the day the house was as spick and span as if she had cleaned it herself. Magnus had even made a potful of stovies, not as tasty as Gran's but good enough. When Mr Skinnymalink came in, sniffing the appetizing smell, Magnus knew better than to ask if he would share the meal. He just fetched an extra platter from the dresser and ladled out another helping.

The Hermit ate in his usual abstracted manner, but at the end of the meal he smacked his lips and said, 'That was good.'

Magnus felt pleased. It was not often Mr Skinnymalink made a comment, about food or anything else. He cleared away the plates and brewed the tea in Gran's big brown pot. Then the pair of them sat drinking in silence.

When the Hermit pushed back his chair and rose to go, he spoke to Magnus in his croaky voice. 'There are still two sheep across on Little Sula. We can fetch them tomorrow, if you like.'

'Right,' said Magnus gratefully. He was well aware of the work Mr Skinnymalink had already done to help Gran. The hen-house roof had been patched up, the fence mended, and many an odd job done. It was the Hermit's way of thanking the old woman who had so often fed and cared for him in the past.

'How is the teacher?' Magnus asked, as Mr Skinnymalink was going out of the door.

'Andrew? He's gone off his head.'

'What?' said Magnus, looking alarmed. 'Is he ill?'

'Mad!' The Hermit screwed up his face. 'He says he's going to get married. Idiot! He can think of nothing else but sprucing up the house and getting everything shipshape. I can tell you something, Magnus, I'm not going to stay there once he brings a woman into the place. I'll go back to my cave, that's what I'll do.'

It was the longest speech Magnus had ever heard him make. He looked so agitated that the boy did his best to soothe him down.

'But she's nice, Mr Skinnymalink. Diana. You'll get on fine with her.'

'No, I won't,' said the Hermit, stubbornly. 'I don't like changes.' He looked sadly across to Little Sula, as if he wished he could go and live there, out of touch with every living soul.

'It'll be all right, Mr Skinnymalink. You'll see.'

'Huh!' said Mr Skinnymalink, and went on his way, kicking a stone, like a cross schoolboy.

Magnus felt some sympathy for him. He had no liking for changes, himself. But this one, surely, would be a change for the better. And the main thing was, the schoolmaster would be content and happy. Doubtless the Hermit would hide away in his cave for a time, but Magnus guessed it would not be for long before Diana found a way to win him over.

Next day, as the boy worked in the house and outside on the croft, he began to realize fully how hard Gran's daily life had been. How often he had seen her bearing bundles of hay in her arms, struggling to carry heavy pails, or kneeling to scrub the kitchen floor. It was not till he tackled all the tasks himself that he realized the full extent of her labours. Little wonder that after a lifetime of such exertion Gran had at last begun to feel the strain. He was thankful he was young and strong enough to shoulder the burden.

Mr Skinnymalink was still in a morose mood when they rowed across to Little Sula. Not a word did he say, only grunted now and again as he tugged at the oars. Magnus knew better than to take any notice of him. He was searching the water for a sight of Old Whiskers.

Suddenly he saw the seal lolling about on the surface of the water looking as doleful as the Hermit; but the creature soon cheered up when it caught sight of the boat, and came flapping towards it, making sounds of pleasure.

'Hullo, Old Whiskers, I'm home!' cried Magnus, leaning over the boat and patting his old friend on the snout. 'It's great to see you again.'

The seal reared himself up, turned a clumsy somersault and almost landed in the boat. Then he disappeared below the surface, content in the knowledge that the boy was there.

'Seals are all right,' said the Hermit, breaking his silence. 'But women!'

On Little Sula Magnus went and stood in the middle of the Fairy Ring before helping to round up the black-faced sheep. He wanted to wish a wish, about a woman. Not Diana, but Gran.

'Make her well and let her come home soon.'

He looked up into the sky and saw a solitary bird flying overhead. A solan goose with its neck outstretched, winging its way over the little island. A bird of good omen. Magnus felt cheered as he watched it. It was a sign, he felt sure, that his wishes would come true.

Back home, he took the sheep up to the Heathery Hill where Sheltie came running towards him, nuzzling against his neck.

'Come on then, Sheltie, I'll ride you home,' said the boy, leaping on to the pony's back. On the way they met the District Nurse, back at work after her illness, riding her wobbly bicycle.

'Are you all right, Magnus?' she called out.

'Uh-huh! I'm fine.'

'Have you heard the news about the schoolmaster getting married? Fancy! A bride on the island.' She sighed. 'I wish *I* had the chance! Ah well, there's always work. I'll be keeping an eye on your Gran when she comes back.'

'Me, too,' said Magnus.

Gran had been keeping her eye on too many people in the past. Now it was his turn to see that she looked after herself.

The Cowans, the McCallums and all the other neighbours kept asking him in for meals. But Magnus wanted to be left to fend for himself, not to take the easy way out. He must stand on his own feet.

He had made his first attempt at baking scones. They had turned out doughy, burnt on the outside and uncooked in the middle. Magnus ate them with a chunk of cheese – waste-not-want-not – and resolved to try again the next day. By the time Gran came home he would have mastered the art of making pancakes as well as learned to churn butter, and even to darn his own stockings. Anything to lighten her load.

The winter day was short. It had grown dark early and

the lamp was lit. At the end of his meal Magnus's head
began to nod and he felt ready for bed. But he pulled
himself up when he heard a rattle of pebbles against
the window-pane. The Ferret's calling-card! Reluctantly
Magnus rose to his feet and went outside.

The air was as sharp as a knife-edge and the frosted
ground crackled like broken glass beneath his feet. It was
the only sound to be heard except for a sudden hiss from
the Ferret, lurking in a nearby doorway.

'Pssssst! Is that you, Magnus?'

'Uh-huh!' said Magnus warily.

There had been no time for their usual fights, and he
knew the Ferret was feeling neglected. What mischief was
he up to now?

'I've got a message from thon man.'

'What man?'

'Him! The schoolmaster. You've to go and see him as
soon as you can.'

'Right, I'll come.'

'Teacher's pet!' scoffed the Ferret, trying to trip
Magnus up. Then, in his gruff voice, he said, 'I've got
something to show you.'

'What?' asked Magnus, suspiciously.

The Ferret fell into step beside him and drew

something from his pocket, small and furry, quivering with fear. Magnus could feel the rapid heartbeats as he held the creature in his hand.

'It's only a wee mouse,' said the Ferret. 'I thought we could put it through somebody's door. Maybe old Morag's, to give her a fright.'

'No!' said Magnus fiercely, concerned more for the mouse than for old Morag who could easily enough deal with it.

'I'll let it away.' He set the mouse down on the ground and it went scampering off with a frightened squeak.

'Och you! You're soft!' cried the Ferret, lunging out at him. 'Are you on for a fight?'

'No, I'm not!'

'Huh!' The Ferret pushed him away in disgust. 'I'm fed up.' He was about to shuffle off when he had second thoughts and turned back. 'I've got something else in my pocket,' he said in a sheepish voice. 'It's for Gran.'

It was a boy's handkerchief, grubby from lying about in the Ferret's pocket in company with field-mice, catapults, safety-pins and chewing gum. But it was neatly folded and unused. It had been a present at Christmas – one of his few personal possessions – and now he wanted to pass it on to Gran. The old woman, in spite of her sharp tongue, had often stood up for him when he was in a tight corner. They had a certain respect for each other, and this was the only way the Ferret could think of showing his feelings.

'Okay,' said Magnus, taking the present in the spirit in which it was offered. 'I'll send it to her.' But he would take it home and wash it first. 'I'll fight you tomorrow,' he shouted after the Ferret. It was *his* way of saying thank you.

Magnus noticed the change in the schoolhouse the

moment he entered it. New curtains, coloured cushions, some pictures on the wall, and Diana's photograph on the mantelpiece.

The teacher himself was looking brighter, sitting by the fireside with Trix on the rug at his feet. A book was balanced on his knees but he was not reading it. His eyes were straying more often to the photograph.

Mr Skinnymalink was sitting at the table with his back turned to him, whittling away at a piece of wood and muttering crossly to himself. He paid no attention to Magnus when he came in, but Andrew Murray sprang to his feet with a pleased look on his face.

'Magnus! Come in. It's good to see you. How is your grandmother?'

'She'll be home soon,' said Magnus, stooping to pat the little dog. 'What did you want?'

'Want? Oh yes! I wanted you to look at this book.' He limped across and laid it on the table. 'Sit down, Magnus, and see what you think of it.'

The Hermit huddled over his work without looking up, while Magnus turned the pages of the old book which the teacher had been looking at. It was a book about the big beasts. Magnus did not read the text but he studied the faded illustrations. So that was what a brontosaurus looked like! And a pterodactyl. He longed to put more life into the pictures so that they would look real and not stuffed.

The teacher gave him a sidelong look. 'You could do a great deal better, couldn't you, Magnus? And I could try to write a more interesting story. Perhaps we could do another book together.'

'Uh-huh!' said Magnus. 'We might.'

'Good!' said Andrew with a satisfied note in his voice. It was another small victory for him, another step forward. 'Perhaps Diana might have a hand in it, too. She knows more about the subject than I do. The three of us could work together.'

The Hermit gave a grunt of distaste, while Magnus asked, 'When are you thinking of getting married?'

'I'm thinking of it all the time,' smiled Andrew. 'In the spring. I hope. Then we'll have the long summer in Sula to look forward to.' He smiled with happiness at the prospect, then turned to the boy. 'What about you, Magnus? When will you be going back to the High School?'

'I'm not going back. Not as long as Gran needs me.'

Andrew Murray saw the stubborn look on the boy's face and knew the signs, but he could not stop himself from crying out, 'But what about your drawing and painting lessons? You must not give them up, Magnus. You're making such good progress . . .'

'Goodnight!' said Magnus, rising hastily to his feet and going out without another word.

Andrew pushed aside the book while Mr Skinnymalink gave him a look as much as to say, 'See!'

The teacher was left, as he had so often been before, with the feeling that an eel had slipped through his fingers. It was always the same with Magnus. One step forward and another back.

Next day Magnus baked a batch of pancakes. Drop-scones, Gran called them. He was pleased with the result as he set them on a wire tray to cool.

'Not bad,' he thought, and wished that Gran herself was here to taste them. He was keeping a watchful eye on Specky and Rebecca who were both trying to jump on to the table, when he heard a fumbling at the door.

It was Tair, muffled up against the cold, and with some great news to impart.

'D'you know what Avizandum says? There's a boat coming.'

'Avizandum's talking nonsense,' said Magnus, handing him one of the hot pancakes. 'The *Hebridean*'s not due for another three days.'

'It's not the *Hebridean*,' said Tair, chewing at his pancake. 'Come and see.'

Magnus went out to humour the small boy; but when he looked towards the sea he stood still with surprise. There coming towards the pier, was a boat: *The Maid of Cronan*.

'See!' said Tair. 'Avizandum's always right.'

The Maid was not filled with tourists. Who would come jaunting to Sula on a cold winter's day? Indeed, there seemed to be only two passengers on board. The Duke and Gran.

Magnus ran helter-skelter towards the pier, taking great jumps for joy into the air. If he had been wearing a hat he would have thrown it high above his head. Gran looked so like herself, standing stiff and straight, not even hanging on to the rail. The Duke was waving wildly and calling, 'Hullo, boy! Couldn't wait for the *Hebridean*, so I chartered *The Maid*. What d'you think of that?'

'Great!' cried Magnus, and leapt on board without waiting for the gangway to be lowered. 'Welcome home, Gran.'

He took hold of her rough hand and clung to it. 'Hullo, laddie,' she said, but she did not look at him. She was gazing around her at all the sights of Sula, as if drinking them in. The row of cottages, the church, the school, the winding road that led to the Heathery Hill. Magnus and the Duke tried to help her down the gangway but she shook them off.

'I'll manage myself,' she said, in her old independent way.

The news had spread and the people came running out when they heard the boat had arrived. Old Cowan raised a cheer, but Gran did not linger long to speak to any of them. With the Duke and Magnus beside her, she marched straight towards her own cottage and shut the door. She was home.

She took a quick look round at the clean kitchen, the bright fire, the scrubbed floor, the dusted shelves, and at the pancakes on the table. Then she gave a sigh of satisfaction and turned to Magnus. 'You've done well, laddie,' she told him.

Magnus flushed with pleasure, then he looked at her anxiously and drew forward a chair. 'Sit down, Gran.'

'What for?'

Gran was already searching for her apron in the dresser drawer.

'You've got to rest,' Magnus told her.

'That's right,' agreed the little Duke. 'Remember what the doctor said. Plenty of rest, and take your pills every day.'

'Pills!' scoffed Gran, tying on her apron defiantly. But she sat down and waited till Magnus made the tea and buttered some of the pancakes. He watched while she ate, waiting on tenterhooks for the verdict.

'I'd like another,' she said, stretching out her hand; and Magnus knew that he had passed the test.

The Duke was making signs for him to go outside. 'A word in your ear, Magnus,' he said when they were on the doorstep. 'The boat's waiting. Do you want to come back with me to Cronan?'

'And leave Gran? No, Duke; I'll stay here.'

'Right!' The little man made no attempt to change Magnus's mind. 'Look after yourself, boy. We'll talk about the future later.'

'Thanks, Duke!'

The future could take care of itself. Nothing mattered to Magnus now that Gran was safely home.

10 Drama in Sula

Spring had come to Sula and everything looked new and fresh. The grass was green, the sea sparkled, and there was a feeling of renewed life and energy in the air.

Too much energy in the Ferret's case. The boy was in trouble. Real trouble. This was more than a mere boyish prank. If there had been a policeman on the island the Ferret would have been in jail by now. Or so the Reverend Morrison said.

It all began with the ringing of the church bell.

'On Wednesday!' cried the minister, hurrying out of the Manse gate and round to the church to see what was happening.

It was the Ferret, of course, up to his tricks. The Devil, according to His Reverence, had got into the restless boy. The Ferret had already been in trouble that day on several counts: for running away from school, for letting down old Morag's washing line on to the muddy ground, for puncturing the District Nurse's bicycle tyre by sticking a rusty nail into it. It seemed that the minister was right. The Devil was urging the Ferret on to even wickeder ploys.

The startled people came running out when they heard the ding dong of the bell. Could it be an alarm call? The older ones remembered that during the war it was the tolling of the church bell that warned them of an air-raid. What new menace was threatening the island?

The Reverend Alexander Morrison was purple with rage.

'That boy!' he shouted, shaking his fist at the Ferret's disappearing back. 'Wait till I get my hands on him!'

But the Ferret had dodged away from his pursuers, pleased enough with the stir he had caused. He was making his way towards the Heathery Hill, where he intended to hide in the Hermit's cave till the tumult had died down.

Magnus had been out cutting peat when he heard the din.

'After him!' yelled the minister, waving his arms like flails. 'Run, Magnus! You can go faster than the rest of us. Bring that boy back. I'm going to punish him if it's the last thing I do.'

Magnus set off in pursuit, though not wholeheartedly. He had a fellow feeling for the Ferret and was not keen to be the one to bring him to justice. Yet he knew that, sooner or later, the red-headed boy would have to face up to his misdeeds. Magnus decided to give him a run for his money before catching him up and trying to reason with him.

He sped up the hill, scattering the few sheep that browsed amongst the bracken and bog-myrtle. He could see the Ferret loping away ahead of him like a scurrying rabbit. Then suddenly he saw him bend down and swoop something up.

It was old Cowan's gun, the one he used when he was out after rabbits. He had been up on the Heathery Hill when he heard the church bell ringing, and had dropped the gun in alarm before hurrying down to find out what had happened.

In the Ferret's hands the gun became a lethal weapon. He was used to firing off his catapult at anyone who crossed his path. More out of bravado than anything else, he cocked up the gun and aimed it at Magnus.

'Go away, Magnus Macduff, or I'll shoot you!'

'Don't be daft,' shouted Magnus, standing his ground. 'Put that gun down.'

Too late. There was a sharp report that cracked through the air like a whiplash. The Ferret had not really meant to press the trigger, but his reflex actions had taken over, and the dreadful deed was done.

The gun dropped from his hands and he stared at Magnus in horror, surprised and relieved to find him still standing on his feet. The shot had gone wild, but it had hit something. One of Gran's black-faced sheep lay dead in the heather.

At first Magnus was too stunned to speak. Then: 'See what you've done!' he cried out, shocked at the Ferret's crime. 'You've killed a sheep.' He felt no relief that *he* had escaped the same fate. He could only think what the loss of one of her few sheep would mean to Gran.

The Ferret, white-faced and shaken, made no attempt to escape. 'I didn't mean it,' he blurted out, coming forward and bending over the sheep's body. 'It just happened.'

He gazed up at Magnus who glared back at him. Magnus was shaking with rage, yet he did not know what to do. No punishment would be bad enough for the Ferret. Punching him on the nose would not bring Gran's sheep back to life.

The Ferret was waiting to be hit. At that moment he would have welcomed a beating. He would not even have tried to defend himself. But it hurt him more when Magnus turned away without another word and ran off down the hill, leaving him alone with the dead carcass.

Strangely enough, it was Gran herself who was the first to forgive the unhappy Ferret. For days he had lurked about like a stray dog, not daring to show his face in the schoolroom or at the church. Whenever Magnus saw him, he turned away and cut him dead. The Ferret had expected punishment, but this was the worst fate that could have happened to him.

One evening at the gloaming he came slinking towards Gran's door, attracted by the appetizing smell of roast mutton. The dead sheep had been shared around, and every household was having a feast. It was an ill wind that blew nobody any good.

The Ferret was hungry. Not only for food, but for a kind word. He got it from Gran. When the old woman came to the door he shrank back, expecting an angry blow, or at the best a spate of harsh words. Instead, she beckoned him in.

'Come in. The supper's ready.'

The Ferret stared at her unbelievingly. 'S-supper!' he stammered. She was actually inviting him in to eat the sheep he had killed!

The appetizing aroma seemed even more tempting now that the door was open, but the Ferret was too taken aback to accept Gran's surprising invitation. He was about to dart away when she repeated it.

'The supper's ready. Come in. There's plenty.'

The Ferret hesitated. 'What about Magnus?' he asked fearfully.

'He's out milking the cow. It's all right. Come in.'

The Ferret sidled round the door, looking at the clean kitchen, the bright fire, the pot of potatoes, and the meat ready to be dished up. For the last few days he had been living off scraps, and sharing the cave with Mr Skinnymalink who had left the schoolhouse in a huff now that Andrew's marriage was coming nearer. It would be a treat to have a real meal for a change.

'Sit in to the table,' said Gran, serving out a generous helping of the good food. 'Eat up.'

The Ferret looked at his plate, then at Gran. Hungry though he was, he could not eat a bite till he had said something.

'I'm awful sorry,' he burst out.

It was little enough to say, but Gran accepted it. She nodded her head at him and said simply, 'It's past. Eat away.'

He noticed out of the corner of his eye that she had the handkerchief in her apron pocket, the one he had given Magnus to send to her in the hospital. Somehow the sight of it made him feel better, and he began to eat hungrily.

Every mouthful of food made him feel stronger and warmer. But the greatest warmth he felt was for Gran. There was nothing he would not do for her. She had not preached at him, nor hit him, nor said one word of anger, in spite of the terrible thing he had done.

The old woman was carving him another slice of mutton when the door opened. Magnus came in, carrying the milk pail and whistling *Scotland the Brave*. The whistling came to an abrupt stop when he saw the Ferret sitting at the table, tucking in to his supper.

His face flushed with anger and he dumped down the pail on the floor. 'What's *he* doing here?' he cried out to Gran.

'Eating his supper,' said Gran calmly. 'Come and have yours, too, Magnus.'

'Not me,' said Magnus, making for the door. He was not going to sit down beside a murderer.

'Mag-nus!' said Gran in her sternest voice. She gave him a warning glance, but he glowered back at her defiantly and would have flounced out had she not

suddenly held her hand to her heart. 'Fetch my pills,' she said, feebly.

It was not often Gran gave way to such underhand methods. Even now she could not bring herself to lie when Magnus called out in alarm, 'Is your heart bad again, Gran?' and rushed to the cupboard to fetch the bottle of pills.

'No, it's not,' said Gran truthfully. 'I just forgot to take the pills.'

But it had the desired effect on Magnus, who realized there were more important things than the Ferret's misdeeds. He watched anxiously while Gran swallowed the pills, recalling the nurse's warning at Cronan Hospital. No scenes, no excitements, no stresses or strains. And if

111

Gran had forgiven the Ferret, maybe he should give in, too.

'Sit in to your supper,' said Gran, placing his plate on the table. 'It's all past, and he's sorry.'

'He had better be!' muttered Magnus; but he sat down beside the Ferret and took the food Gran put before him. The Ferret gave him a sidelong glance, unsure whether to continue eating or not. But when Gran gave him a reassuring nod, he took another mouthful and the meal continued in silence.

At the end Magnus pushed back his chair, and for the first time for days spoke to the Ferret.

'Come on out and I'll fight you.' It was his way of letting bygones be bygones.

'Right!' said the Ferret, beaming from ear to ear.

It was great! Life had returned to normal.

The Ferret never forgot the debt he owed to Gran. From that day on he would run any distance to come to her aid. 'Is there anything I can do for you?' he was constantly asking her. His efforts were sometimes clumsy, but there was no doubt about his willingness.

It was Gran who suggested he might make amends to the minister. Obeying her orders, he went secretly and patched up the broken-down wall round the Manse garden. He even ventured inside to weed the rockery, keeping a wary eye on the door in case His Reverence came out.

Of course, the Ferret's finer feelings did not last. It was not long before he was in trouble again. But he never forgot Gran's kindness. She had made him her slave for life; and in this she was not as innocent as she seemed.

For Gran had a plan. She was feeling better. Her heart was stronger, and the District Nurse had said, 'You'll outlive the lot of us, as long as you remember to take care, and get somebody to help with the heavy work.'

Magnus had done his bit willingly, and with no grumbles. What was there to grumble about? This was the life he liked best, running wild in Sula and helping Gran. He even went willingly to school each day, though more often he sat doodling dinosaurs on his jotter than listening to Andrew Murray trying to teach the class geography. He was content to go on like this for ever, swimming with the seals, riding the Shetland pony, rowing across to Little Sula, and being Gran's right-hand man.

It was a letter from Lionel that opened Gran's eyes. The London boy was writing to Magnus to tell him about the progress he was making with his singing lessons.

'I'm learning such a lot. Singing in a choir, studying opera, and there's a chance that I might get into the Academy of Music,' wrote Lionel, full of enthusiasm. 'All thanks to the Duke. How are you getting on with your drawing, Magnus? You have a wonderful talent. I was thinking of you the other day when I went into one of the galleries. I had a vision which I am sure will come true. I knew there would be a *Magnus Macduff* on the walls one day, hanging beside the famous paintings. So, keep on, Magnus. There's such a lot to learn . . .'

Magnus himself did not pay much heed to the letter; but after Gran read it she furrowed her brows and sat thinking. Then she made up her mind. That evening she put a barley-bannock and some brown eggs in a basket to take to the teacher.

She found him sprucing up the house, making final preparations to receive his bride. The Easter holidays were at hand, and Andrew would soon be off to the mainland for his wedding.

Gran was not one for idle chat. She dumped down the basket and came straight to the point:

'Mr Murray, it's time that boy went away. He should go back to Cronan and get on with his training.'

It was what Andrew had been thinking himself. 'But how will you manage without him?' he asked Gran.

'Fine.' The old woman straightened her back. 'The Ferret will help me. The Duke's coming over for the Easter holidays, so Magnus had better go back with him. Will you have a word with the laddie, Mr Murray?'

'I'll try. It's for the boy's own good.' But it would not be as easy as all that to persuade Magnus.

Easter had come, and so had Jinty Cowan, home for the holidays. She had followed Magnus up the Heathery Hill where he had gone in search of Sheltie. She was still wearing her school uniform so that everyone in Sula could see what a superior young lady she had become. Now that she had been out into the big world, she knew more than the entire population of the island put together.

But there was one thing she did not know. Magnus had agreed to go back to the mainland after the holidays. How pleased she would be when she heard!

The Duke had not tried to persuade him one way or another, except to say wistfully, 'It's lonely in the Tower. I'm getting on with my music, but it helps when you're there, boy, doing your drawing.' He sighed. 'The castle seems very empty without you.'

It was Andrew Murray who made Magnus see that the right thing to do would be to go back to Cronan.

'Why not try another term? I promise to send word at once if your grandmother becomes ill. Though she's heaps better and wants you to go.' He was not sure whether Magnus was listening to him, but he went on earnestly. 'She doesn't say much, but I know how proud she is of your pictures, Magnus. You still have a lot to learn and the Art Master at the High School is anxious to have you back. Think it over.'

Still no response from Magnus. Andrew tried again. 'Don't forget that Diana will be here. She'll help to keep an eye on your grandmother,' he said brightly. 'And, of course, you'll be home often, Magnus. I wish you would go. It would be a feather in my cap if a pupil of mine made a success of his life.'

Magnus cared little about success. All the same, he was beginning to feel the itch to learn more about drawing and painting. At the High School he could study the art books in the library, and benefit from the advice of John Craigie, the Art Master. Most of all, he would be helping the lonely little Duke by staying in the castle.

'Will you go, Magnus?' asked Andrew Murray, trying to read the boy's thoughts.

'I might,' said Magnus; but by the time he went up the hill to look for the pony he had made up his mind. He would try it for another term, if Gran could spare him.

Jinty was babbling on about life in Cronan as if it was the capital city of the world. 'It's great! I go to the pictures as often as I can. The fillums. D'you know what, Magnus? I've made up my mind. That's what I'm going to be.'

'What?' asked Magnus idly, catching hold of Sheltie's rough mane. He was looking at Tair and the twins down on the lower slopes, rolling their Easter eggs.

'I'm going to be a fillum star,' said Jinty, fluttering her eyelashes at Magnus.

She was so carried away with the thought that she did

not watch where she put her feet. And carried away she
was in reality, for the next moment Jinty tripped over a
clump of heather, lost her balance and went rolling away
down the hill like one of the Easter eggs. A fallen fillum
star!

11 A Day to Remember

Once more the flag was flying from the topmost tower at Cronan Castle.

The Duke was in residence. So was Magnus Macduff, though he was not inside the castle at the moment but sitting at the top of a monkey-puzzle tree in the untidy grounds.

It was Saturday and he was free from the High School, free from his uniform and into his old kilt. He had climbed up the tree so that he could have a good view of the sea. If he strained his eyes he could almost make himself believe he saw Sula far away on the horizon.

It was the kind of day, bright and sunny, when he might have been swimming with the seals if he had been at home. Or floating on the water with Old Whiskers at his side. A lark was singing in the sky, and he could almost imagine that Gran was calling to him, 'Mag-nus! Bring in the peat. Mag-nus . . .'

He had already been in touch with the island that morning. He had telephoned Gran, though it was not an easy process getting through to her.

He had to wait till Jinty's mother, Mrs Cowan at the Post Office and General Store, had said her say. She was as much of a chatterbox as her daughter.

'So it's yourself, Magnus. And how are you? Is His Grace well? What's the weather like in Cronan? Yes, it's lovely here, but it was a bit windy through the week. The boat had a terrible job getting in to the pier. The McCallum twins were nearly blown off their feet, and the District Nurse—' On and on.

'Could I speak to Gran, please?'

'Yes. Hold on and I'll see if I can find her. I saw her going past the door a wee while ago. Maybe she's away to milk the cow. Hold on, Magnus.'

Magnus held on. All around him in the castle hall hung stags' horns, claymores, battle-axes, faded flags, and portraits of the Duke's ancestors. But he did not see them. He was looking out of the open door, visualizing Gran milking the cow. Would the Ferret be there, waiting to carry the heavy pail? And who would be reminding Gran to take her pills?

'Hullo!'

Gran's voice sounded severe on the telephone.

'Is that you, Gran?'

'Yes.'

'How are you?'

'Fine.'

A pause, then Gran said, 'Are you all right, Magnus?'

'Uh-huh!'

It was always the same. When he was away from Gran he could think of a hundred things to say to her, but the moment they met face to face or spoke on the telephone, he became as dumb as a dyke.

He racked his brains. 'Is everything okay, Gran?' he asked.

'Yes.' Another pause. 'The Ferret's helping.'

'That's good.' Yet Magnus felt a stab of jealousy, the same he had felt about Lionel. Was the Ferret replacing him in Gran's eyes?

'Mag-nus!' This time she sounded more like herself.

'Yes, Gran.'

'You'll be back soon?' There was a wistful note in her voice that drove away all the feelings of jealousy.

'Yes, Gran, as soon as I can. Take care of yourself.'

'The same to you, laddie.'

It was not much of a conversation, but it gave the boy a feeling of satisfaction, as he sat perched at the top of the tree. Looking down, he could see old Dan waging war on the nettles in the undergrowth. Later, he would go down and help him, though it was a losing battle. It would have taken a dozen or more active men to keep the castle grounds in order, but the Duke could not afford to employ them. Though his finances had improved since the success of the *Sula Symphony*, which was selling all over the world, the money was soon swallowed up by the backlog of bills waiting to be paid.

'Never mind, boy; I'll write more music and we'll be millionaires some day,' the little man had said, sitting on the stool in his cluttered Tower room. 'And wait till you paint a real picture. That'll make our fortunes.'

Magnus had already painted a real picture, the first he had attempted on a large canvas. He had benefited from the Art Master's advice at the High School and from the picture books he had studied in the library. Because of this, his work had taken on an added dimension. He had widened his scope, but it was still Sula that had inspired him.

The picture was full of brilliantly observed detail, down to the smallest footprints of seabirds on the Sula sands. It was a peaceful picture to gaze at and never become weary of seeing. It was the first he had signed – *Magnus Macduff* – with a faint feeling of pride.

'It's not too bad,' he thought, and left it there on the easel.

For some reason he felt shy of showing it to the little Duke. But His Grace had wandered into the boy's room one day and stood riveted in front of the picture. Words seemed to fail him. He shook hands solemnly with

Magnus, then turned and went back to his own room without making any comment; but Magnus sensed that he was pleased.

The little man was spending more and more time shut up in the Tower room. His music occupied most of his thoughts, but he was pleased to know that Magnus was nearby, even though they spoke little to each other. But today he had called through, 'Clear off, boy. Go out and get some fresh air. I'm expecting some visitors later. Must finish this piece of music first.'

'Right, Duke.'

Magnus was used to the little man's eccentric ways and took himself off without thinking more about it. Maybe it was the London conductor, Sir Ronald Briggs, who was coming. Now he looked down at the peacocks straggling about on the weedy driveway, then gazed idly towards the gates. He gave a start when he saw two figures peering in through the railings. Jinty Cowan and Wee Willy.

Wee Willy was the nearest to a friend that Magnus had at the High School. Very different from the Ferret. Willy was a gentle creature, not able to stand up for himself, the target for all bullies. Magnus kept a protective eye on him, and many a time had saved him from the rough pranks of some of the more boisterous boys.

Wee Willy lived next door to Rockview, the Reekies' house where Jinty was staying. It had not taken her long to make Willy into her doormat. He followed her around like a tame poodle, ready to do her bidding and grateful if she spared him a word or a smile.

It gave Jinty a heady feeling of power to have such a willing slave at her command. If only Magnus would react in the same way!

'Silly wee thing!' thought Magnus, from the top of the tree. 'What's *she* wanting?'

Need he ask? Jinty was wanting a glimpse of *him*. Or, better still, an invitation to come inside and explore the castle. Think what a lot of exciting things she would have to tell the Reekies! Even gazing through the gates was better than nothing. Jinty could make a good story out of very little.

Magnus hesitated. Should he go down and speak to them? Jinty was, after all, someone from Sula; and Wee Willy was his friend. But he would sooner have had the Ferret. He was in the mood for a rough-and-tumble fight.

'Yoo-hoo, Magnus!'

Jinty had spotted him. Maybe her voice would carry and he would come running, overjoyed to find her waiting at the gates. He would invite her in, and the Duke would ask her to stay in the castle. She would occupy the Blue Room, the one kept for royalty. She would sleep in a four-poster bed and eat her supper off a golden plate. Miss Jinty Cowan – no! – *Lady* Jinty Cowan of Cronan Castle.

Magnus came shinning down the tree. He might as well have a word with Wee Willy and the silly little lassie, but he was not going to let them in.

'The Duke's busy. He's not to be disturbed. What are you wanting?' he called, as he made his way towards the gates.

'I just came to say hullo,' said Jinty. She reached out, like a monkey in a cage, to grab his hand. 'If we can't come in, can you not come out?'

'Yes, come on, Magnus,' said Wee Willy. Anything Jinty wanted, *he* wanted.

'Okay, then,' said Magnus, 'but just for a wee while.'

They went and sat on a grassy knoll opposite the castle, overlooking the sea. Jinty gave a romantic sigh. It would be great to have her picture taken here, sitting between her two swains and with the Duke's castle in the

background. She moved closer to Magnus but he did not notice. He was gazing across the sea, wondering what Gran was doing in Sula. The last time he had seen her she was wearing his brooch on her blouse, the one he had brought back from London. The lover's knot.

Jinty was making a daisy-chain. Wee Willy ran to and fro, gathering the daisies for her, glad to be able to help. Jinty accepted his service as if it were her due, and when the daisy-chain was long enough she flung it round Magnus's neck.

'There! You look great!'

'Silly thing!' said Magnus, pulling it off and thrusting it back at her.

Jinty put it round her own neck and asked, 'Does it suit me?'

'Oh yes!' said Wee Willy, gazing at her with dog-like devotion. 'You look lovely, Jinty.'

'Oh well!' she sighed. It was a pity the compliment had not come from Magnus.

Magnus's attention was elsewhere. He had heard the sound of McTear's taxi, the local rattletrap, nearing the castle gates. Turning round, he caught a glimpse of the occupants. A man who looked like Sir Ronald Briggs, the famous conductor from London, and another sitting beside him, smoking a cigar.

'Is it some of the Royal Family?' asked Jinty, all agog.

'No,' scoffed Magnus. He rose and stretched himself. 'Come on for a walk.' Sitting still and making daisy-chains was not his idea of fun.

They walked along the pebbly shore side by side, Jinty in the middle. She would have liked to take hold of Magnus's hand, but that would have been going too far. It was blissful enough to be walking beside him, with Wee Willy at her other side, breathing heavily. She chattered

123

away to Magnus, getting little response but an occasional 'Uh-huh!' He was happy enough, listening to a lark singing in the sky and watching the waves tumbling in to the shore. It was not Sula, of course, but it was the same sea, with the gulls wheeling overhead and the seaweed slithering under his feet.

'I wish it was the summer holidays,' said Jinty, feeling the same longing for home. She cast a glance at Wee Willy. 'Would you like to come?'

Wee Willy went bright pink with pleasure. 'To Sula? Oh, yes!' He was so overcome at the thought that he stood stock still and hugged himself with joy.

'Wheesht!' said Magnus suddenly. 'Do you hear something?'

Clang-clang. Clang-clang.

'It's a bell,' said Jinty, cocking her head to one side like a sparrow.

'I'll have to go,' said Magnus. They wandered back towards the castle gates and he could see Bella on the doorstep, ringing the cracked dinner bell to attract his attention. 'The Duke wants me.'

Jinty sighed. A pity the Duke did not want *her*.

'I'll see you soon again, Magnus?' she said hopefully. 'You'll maybe come and visit me at the Reekies?'

'Maybe I will.'

He turned and looked at her. The ready tears were beginning to well up in her eyes and drip down like raindrops on to her rosy cheeks. Instant emotion. Yet there was something about her that touched a spot in his heart. She was Jinty Cowan, a silly wee lassie, but part of his life in Sula. On a sudden impulse he gave her hand a squeeze, and left her in the seventh heaven with Wee Willy standing patiently by her side.

*

'America! What d'you think of that, boy?'

'Mercy me!' said Magnus, dumbfounded.

America was the next place beyond Sula, but it was hundreds and hundreds of miles away. Almost as far off as the moon. Magnus had often looked in that direction and wondered what it was like, away beyond the horizon. But he had never dreamed that he would visit it. Even now he could not believe it. The Duke often talked a lot of daft nonsense.

'It's true,' said the little man in an excited voice. 'But that's not the best of it, boy. Let me introduce you to Mr Goodfellow. Mr Elmer P. Goodfellow from New York.'

They were up in the Tower room, surrounded by the untidy muddle of the Duke's schoolboy treasures. The little man was perched on his favourite stool, with sheets of music strewn at his feet. Sir Ronald Briggs sat on the sagging sofa beside the sprawling dogs, and the smell of cigar smoke drifted through from Magnus's own room where Mr Goodfellow appeared in the doorway. A fat, friendly-looking man who gazed at Magnus with an interested expression on his face.

'Say, are you Magnus Macduff? I sure am pleased to meet you. I have been admiring that picture of yours next door. Is it for sale? I'd sure like to take it back with me.'

Magnus blinked his eyes while the Duke whispered in his ear, 'Mr Goodfellow is a picture dealer. Buys and sells. Guess how much he's going to offer, boy!'

Magnus made no attempt at guessing. It was the painting of the picture that mattered, not the buying or selling. Yet the money might come in useful to buy Gran another black-faced sheep. Or maybe a good coat to keep the old woman warm in winter.

The men were talking over his head about sums of money. Elmer P. Goodfellow was calling him a young genius, but Magnus was hardly listening. He had heard the telephone shrilling down below. Presently old Bella came puffing up the stairs calling, 'Telephone!'

'I'm not in,' the Duke called back.

'It's not for you, Your Grace. It's for Magnus. Somebody from Sula.'

It was bad news! Magnus's face went as white as a sheet, and all thoughts of money and success vanished from his mind. The one thing that mattered was Gran. Had she taken another heart-attack?

He plunged out of the room, almost knocking the Duke off his stool, and rushed headlong down the stairs, jumping them three at a time. His hand was shaking when he reached the hall and took up the receiver.

'H-Hullo,' he said in a trembling voice.

'Is that you, Magnus?'

'Yes, it's me.'

At first he did not recognize the voice at the other end. Low, soft and sweet.

'It's Diana speaking.'

Diana! The schoolmaster's new wife. Mrs Murray. What dread news was she about to impart? Magnus clung to the hall table and hardly dared ask the question: 'What's up?'

'Everything's fine.' There was a comforting sound in Diana's soft voice. 'I just wanted to say hullo to you, Magnus, and let you know how much I am enjoying life in Sula and looking forward to seeing you in the holidays. Oh! Andrew asked me to tell you that the publishers are interested in that book. The one about the big beasts, as you call them.'

Magnus hardly took in what she was saying. He was not thinking of the big beasts. Only of Gran.

'Are you still there, Magnus?'

'Uh-huh!' A pause. 'Is Gran all right?'

'Yes, she's fine,' said Diana cheerfully. 'I don't know how I would get on without her. She's teaching me all sorts of things, how to bake and mend and run the house. I've just seen her, striding along as fit as a fiddle. The Ferret helps her a lot, and I keep my eye on her, too. So there's no need to worry, Magnus. But, of course, she misses you. She was telling me how much she looks forward to seeing you in the holidays.'

The colour came back into Magnus's cheeks. He felt a sudden lift of elation as if he was floating in mid-air. But there seemed to be a frog in his throat when he tried to speak to Diana.

'Tell her . . . tell her . . .'

'Yes, Magnus, I'll tell her,' said Diana in an understanding voice. *She* would know what to say.

Magnus did not go back to join the men upstairs. He ran out into the untidy grounds and shinned up the monkey-puzzle tree. He sat there thinking. Not about America, not about his paintings, not about money or success. Only about Sula and the summer holidays.

If he narrowed his eyes he could see a seal popping up out of the water.

'Hullo, Old Whiskers. I'll soon be home.'

Lavinia Derwent
Sula 45p

Lessons seem silly to Magnus, who lives on the tiny island of Sula.
His first friends are the seals, whom he loves to sketch, especially
Whiskers who will come out of the sea to him. After the seals comes
Skinnymalink the old hermit; and then the other people start to
grow more important to him.

The Boy from Sula 45p

Magnus finds himself in danger when he tries to frustrate the plans
of property developers who threaten the island.

Penelope Lively
The Wild Hunt of Hagworthy 40p

Lucy goes to stay with her aunt in a village where they are reviving
the ancient 'Horn Dance', to raise money for the Church. The
revival begins as a kind of joke but as the days get hotter and hotter
Lucy realizes that there is an underlying sinister tone, and that she
must do something about it before it is too late. Rumour has it that
the Wild Hunt has been heard again – ghost hounds and antlered
horsemen – brought back by the revival of the Horn Dance.

The Driftway 40p

When Paul runs away from home, he travels along the Driftway, an
ancient route between Banbury and Northampton. He soon
discovers that this road has messages for those who can hear them.
The words he hears and the people he encounters have a very
special meaning for him.

You can buy these and other Piccolo books from booksellers and
newsagents; or direct from the following address:
Pan Books, Cavaye Place, London SW10 9PG
Send purchase price plus 20p for the first book and 10p for
each additional book, to allow for postage and packing
Prices quoted are applicable in UK

While every effort is made to keep prices low, it is sometimes
necessary to increase prices at short notice. Pan Books reserve the
right to show on covers new retail prices which may differ
from those advertised in the text or elsewhere